MEG'S
CONFESSION

Other books by Sierra Donovan:

Love on the Air

MEG'S
CONFESSION

•

Sierra Donovan

AVALON BOOKS
NEW YORK

Published by Thomas Bouregy & Co., Inc.
160 Madison Avenue, New York, NY 10016

Library of Congress Cataloging-in-Publication Data

Donovan, Sierra.
    Meg's confession / Sierra Donovan.
        p.   cm.
    ISBN-13: 978-0-8034-9812-9 (hardcover : alk. paper)
    ISBN-10: 0-8034-9812-8 (hardcover : alk. paper)
    1. Widows—Fiction.   2. Pregnant women—Fiction.
    I. Title.

PS3604.O5674M44   2007
813'.6—dc22

                                                2006028587

PRINTED IN THE UNITED STATES OF AMERICA
ON ACID-FREE PAPER
BY HADDON CRAFTSMEN, BLOOMSBURG, PENNSYLVANIA

To Mom, who loved me even when I was impossible.
(Did I say 'was'?)

And to Ninny, who put me out on the porch,
in the rain, when I threatened
to run away from home.

I love you both.

The Joshua Center portrayed in this book was inspired by Moses House, a High Desert crisis pregnancy center that helps women become self-sufficient so that they can be better mothers to their children. I have deep respect and admiration for the work they do. However, the characters depicted in the story have no resemblance to anyone affiliated with Moses House.

Chapter One

Megan Reilly was drifting out of sleep Saturday morning when Jimmy kicked her.

She didn't open her eyes. Lying on her side, she slid one hand between the mattress and her swelling stomach. A few seconds later, it came again: that unmistakable jolt, this time just below her palm. Meg shifted her hand to feel the movement of the baby inside her and smiled.

This was the best time of the day. Just her and Jimmy.

She let the kicking and rolling go on for a minute or so before she opened her eyes and saw the empty half of the double bed. Still just her and Jimmy.

She didn't like to look at Ron's vacant side of the bed for very long. But she had to turn toward it while she slept, or her right arm fell asleep. Carpal tunnel syndrome, the doctor had told her, a pregnancy side effect that would probably disappear after the baby was born.

Meg closed her eyes to shut out the sight of the

1

empty pillow and was hit with another inescapable memory. Last night, when she almost ran into Mrs. Langley from the church she used to go to with Ron, she'd had to duck down the next aisle in the layette section of Target. The last place in the world she wanted to be caught. She didn't want to face the gushed congratulations. Or the questions.

She'd gotten out of the store unnoticed, but it had been a rude awakening.

Jimmy prodded her again, and she couldn't help but laugh at his insistence.

"Okay, sweetie. Time for breakfast."

She knew the baby couldn't consciously communicate, but there were times when he came through loud and clear. Meg wondered if women ever missed the baby inside them once the child was actually born. For her, Jimmy was a constant companion. His activity fascinated her. And, of course, you were supposed to talk to your unborn baby, to help start the bonding.

Meg didn't mind that a bit. It gave her someone to talk to.

But maybe it was time to talk to someone else.

She braced her hands against the mattress to hoist herself into a sitting position. Getting her new girth out of bed grew trickier as the pregnancy progressed. But, seven months in, she was learning.

She swung her legs over the side of the mattress and got up to fix them breakfast.

* * *

Meg pulled up to the curb in front of the little Catholic church in the older part of town. She'd gotten into the habit of driving by it these past several months, but until today, she'd never stopped here.

Things had been quiet this afternoon at the crisis pregnancy center where Meg volunteered two days a week; no one minded when she left a little earlier than usual. The church's listing in the Yellow Pages had said confession was held Saturday afternoon from three-thirty to four-thirty.

Meg had never been inside a Catholic church. But if confession was good for the soul—she needed it.

Still in her car, she looked up the concrete steps leading to the worn double doors of the church. The building probably dated back to the twenties, or even earlier. Somehow, the church's weathered stones and slightly rundown appearance made it seem more inviting. It wasn't an imposing gothic cathedral, but today it loomed taller than before. She gulped in a deep breath and forced herself to stop stalling.

Meg opened the door and got out, sliding her growing stomach carefully out from under the steering wheel. Funny, finding a parking space right in front of the church during confession time. There must be a parking lot behind the building, but this spot offered a quick exit. It might come in handy.

At the top of the stairs, Meg took another shaky breath, pulled open one of the wooden doors, and entered foreign territory.

It was so quiet. Directly ahead of her was another set of dark wood double doors, beautifully carved with intricate scrollwork. Undoubtedly, they led into the church's main sanctuary. She was pretty sure confession wouldn't be done in there, so she turned down a hallway to her right.

There they were. She recognized the confessionals from the movies—those little booths with a separate door on each side. She came to one with a door closed on one side; she detected the sound of movement behind it. One more deep breath, and Meg ducked into the other half before she lost her courage.

"Hello?" came a male voice from the other side.

She didn't allow herself to breathe this time. She began, the way she'd seen in the movies: "Forgive me Father, for I have sinned. . . ."

On the other side of the confessional, Craig Stovall nearly dropped his screwdriver.

He stared at the wall between the two sides of the little booth. Well, it wasn't a vandal, that was for sure. But it was definitely someone who didn't know the church was closed for renovations. He'd come in without his crew today, just to finish up on the hinges.

He opened his mouth to explain, but no words came out.

The earnest woman's voice rushed on, unprompted. "It's been—oh, what am I talking about? I've never been to confession, Father. I'm not even Catholic."

That's okay. Neither am I. No, not the right thing to say. Craig fumbled for something better.

"I guess I just wanted someone to talk to," she went on. "I haven't been to church since I found out I was pregnant. . . ."

This was getting too personal, too fast. Craig cleared his throat. "You—this—" The words came out half–strangled.

Maybe that was why she didn't seem to hear him. "It was bad enough after my husband died. I mean, every-one at the church was so nice, but—every time they looked at me, I knew they were seeing the noble widow. And it's not like that." Her voice was getting more emotional, her words more rushed. "We had a fight the day before he died—"

Craig squirmed. He felt like a peeping Tom. But he couldn't see any way to cut her off now. He'd already let it go on too long.

"He didn't want the baby."

She crammed the words into the smallest space pos-sible. It made the silence that followed seem that much bigger. As the gap stretched out, Craig was sure she was fighting tears.

He clenched his teeth, held his breath, and wished for the worn carpet under his feet to swallow him up.

He expected her to dissolve into sobs, but when she spoke again, her voice was controlled. "We were pack-ing for him to fly out when he brought it up. We'd been trying to have a baby, and he said it was just as well I hadn't gotten pregnant. He said with this kind of a lifestyle, we might as well forget it. I didn't tell him I might already be pregnant, but—I said a lot of other things. I was mad. Of all the times for *him* to decide we shouldn't have a baby—" Craig heard some of the anger still in her voice "—he waits until he's just about to fly out on a three-month assignment." Her voice grew softer. "And then his plane never makes it there."

Craig's brain made a series of rapid-fire connections. Someone named Ron, on a plane that never made it there. Ron Reilly? Of course. It had to be. He'd been an Air Force pilot, a home-town boy. Craig had gone to the same high school with him, though they'd never really known each other. Football jocks like Ron didn't hang out with wood shop kids like Craig. After graduation, Craig kept pounding nails and slowly turned his one visible talent into a self-sufficient business.

Meanwhile, Ron Reilly enlisted in the Air Force, flying all over the world until he finally returned to the base here in Victory, the conquering hero. Only to have his plane crash on a routine mission a few months after he got stationed back home. It had been all over the *Daily News*. Victory was still a small enough town for that.

The woman had stopped talking, he realized. It was very quiet on the other side of the booth. Good grief, was this the part where he was supposed to say something? He didn't know what sin she thought she'd committed, but Craig was pretty sure it wasn't even in the book.

He couldn't sound like a priest even if he tried. But

she wasn't Catholic; maybe she wouldn't know the difference. Craig ran a finger over the screwdriver in his hand and tried to sound educated and reasonable. No way could he manage pious. "I'm sorry, but I don't see what you think you've done wrong."

"I'm a fraud. I'm supposed to be this saintly widow—"

"Says who?" Uh-oh. Not very priestly. But if she noticed, she didn't say anything. Craig tried for a little common sense. "It isn't wrong to argue with your husband. And you didn't make that plane crash. Your friends would understand—"

"They're not *my* friends." There was a fierce desperation in her tone. "They were his. He grew up out here. We moved here just before he died—I barely know anybody. I can't tell them that . . . that things weren't the way they think they were. When he died, everyone was so sympathetic—I felt like a hypocrite. Like I was lying every time I saw someone who knew him."

There had to be something more here than a simple argument. What he'd heard just wasn't enough to explain the woman's moral quandary. Before he thought better of it, Craig asked, "Is the baby his?"

"Of *course* the baby's his!" she flared back. Then she seemed to remember she was snapping at a priest. At least, as far as she knew. "I'm sorry. It's just—I'm carrying a baby my husband didn't even want. I can't tell anyone that. It's disrespectful to . . ." She trailed off. She was sounding less convincing.

Craig followed his hunch. "There's more to it than that, isn't there?"

There was a piercing silence. Then: "I'm not sure if I really loved him."

Oh, help. Get me out of here. What was he doing playing amateur shrink? He was a guy with a hammer, not a psychotherapist. He'd dug a hole for himself the moment he let her get past "Forgive me Father." Now he was turning it into a trench.

Another of those long silences from the other side. Craig was sure this time he was about to hear a huge, racking sob.

Once again she surprised him. "I thought I was in love with him when we got married," she said with only a hint of a quaver in her voice. "But now I wonder—if maybe he was just a safe place. I'd been on my own a long time." Her words were coming out fast again, so fast he couldn't have gotten a word in edge-wise. "He was solid, he was reliable—and he liked the idea of taking care of me. But I think what that really meant was, he wanted me to take care of him. He didn't want me to get a job—he finally *let* me go to work part-time because I was climbing the walls. Sometimes I think he just wanted someone to pack for him when he went off on temporary duty, and to be there waiting when he got back."

Craig writhed on the narrow seat under him. The confessional had never been roomy, but it was getting smaller all the time.

"And then he died. And—I just don't feel the way I'm supposed to feel."

Another long pause. "Well, I guess that's it." The raw emotion had drained out of her voice. She was done? Could it really be over? "Do you want me to say a Hail Mary or anything?" Her tone was deferential once again.

Craig smiled wryly. "Do you know that prayer?"

"No."

The light at the end of the tunnel glimmered just ahead. A few more words and he was off the hook. But after all he'd let her say, Craig felt a need to make those words count for something. "You say you don't feel the way you're supposed to feel." He tried to remember what his old high school counselor had said. "Feelings aren't right or wrong. It's what you do with them. Right?"

"Right," she agreed, as if under orders. She didn't sound convinced.

Craig tried again. "Maybe you made a mistake. Maybe you got married for the wrong reasons. That doesn't make you a bad person. Right?"

"Right." She sounded only a little less dubious this time.

"So don't be so hard on yourself." It may not be what the Pope himself would say, but Craig thought it was pretty decent advice. And he meant it. Otherwise, the woman was going to make herself crazy. "Now go in peace," he ad-libbed, then cringed. It had sounded right until he heard himself say it.

"Thank you," she said, and he heard the door on the other side of the confessional unlatch. Craig let out an inaudible breath.

He waited until her footsteps echoed some distance down the long hallway before he dared unlatch his own side of the confessional to peer out.

He saw the retreating back of a woman wearing a flame-red jacket. Dark brown hair spilled to just past her shoulders. Below the jacket, she wore a dress or skirt, and from the back, her slim, shapely legs didn't look pregnant at all. Only the slight, awkward totter in her walk gave her away. It was faintly comical, but Craig didn't feel like laughing.

He ducked back in just before she turned the corner out of sight.

He didn't think of himself as very sentimental, but he felt an uneasy pang over what he'd just heard. Why hadn't he interrupted her before she got so far?

Craig had been raised by a single mother himself, and he'd given her a hard time of it. Until she'd remarried. Then he'd made it worse.

The image of the red-jacketed woman returned. Unlike his mom, she was single through no choice of her own. He wouldn't want to trade places with her. She must be miserable about having a baby, with no one to help her take care of it. And growing up without a father—a real father—was the pits. Craig knew that firsthand.

He shook his head. Not a thing he could do about it.

So Craig got back to the job of renovating the confessional.

"We haven't had any customers all morning." Kim, one of Meg's two clerks, smoothed the pair of slacks she was folding, gazed out the window of Rosie's Rags and heaved her best long-suffering sigh. The girl had been suffering for all of forty-five minutes, ever since the little clothing store opened at ten.

"We should get busier around lunchtime," Meg said, although she had her doubts. She should probably talk to Rosie, the owner, about scheduling one less person on Monday mornings. Not only would it save the store money on overhead; there would be one less person to complain.

Stephanie, the other clerk, joined her friend in the familiar chorus. "We'd be a lot busier if the store was in the mall." There was no need to identify the mall by name. There was only one in Victory, California. The only one, in fact, within fifty miles.

Stephanie turned to Meg for confirmation. "Don't you think the store would be busier if they moved it to the mall?"

The girls both looked at Meg expectantly, as if she had the power to pick up the store and transplant it on the spot.

Meg restrained herself from borrowing one of their patented eye rolls. "We'd get more foot traffic at the mall, sure." She watched Stephanie give Kim a triumphant look. "But there are tradeoffs. For one thing, they'd probably charge about three times as much rent."

They looked disappointed, but still only half-comprehending. And why not? Stephanie was nineteen years old, still lived with her parents, and had probably never paid a bill in her life. Kim was eighteen, just out of high school, and had probably never written a check before this year.

Was I ever that young? Meg wondered.

She was only twenty-six, but compared to these two, she felt like a rigid old schoolmarm. Of course, that was her job. As assistant manager at Rosie's Rags, Meg got to play the responsible adult when Rosie wasn't around, making sure the girls didn't spend too much time talking on the phone or trying on the clothes.

The girls. She just couldn't quite think of them as women. They were kids in a way Meg hadn't been, at least not for a long time.

Maybe she hadn't been so different at that, back when she was a teenager in Colorado. She'd worked at a clothing store then too, and most of her paycheck had gone toward clothes. Until, at eighteen, she found herself abruptly on her own.

Kim popped up in front of her, holding one of the store's newest sweaters in front of her. "Can we try on a couple of these?"

Meg gave in with a smile. The tolerant schoolmarm. "Just one. And only one of you at a time."

Kim raced for the dressing room at the back of the store.

Yes, everyone should have a chance to be a kid. She couldn't begrudge them that. At times Meg envied her younger co-workers, with so little on their minds, and flat stomachs to boot. She wondered if she'd ever fit into a pair of jeans again. With two months of pregnancy still to go, her waistline was a distant memory.

Meg wandered toward the back of the store in Kim's wake to straighten some leftover summer clothes on the discount racks. Instead, she caught herself stealing a glance at one of the full-length mirrors just outside the dressing rooms. The pregnancy had become more than evident these past few weeks. Earlier on, she'd taken on the shape of a bowling pin; now she looked more like a light bulb. With her round belly jutting so far out in front of her, she looked ready to topple over. That thought, coupled with a swift kick from Jimmy, brought a smile back to her face. Aside from wearing flattering maternity clothes for the sake of the customers at Rosie's Rags, who did she need to impress?

There were more important things. Like being a mother. This wasn't the way she'd planned it, but she still couldn't find room to regret the fact that she'd gotten pregnant before Ron died. After all, it might never happen again.

It was going to be tough, but she'd been in tough spots before. The baby would be worth it. As she'd just told the girls, there were trade-offs.

She could sidestep the self-pity. Now, if she could just find her way past the guilt.

Don't be so hard on yourself.

The priest's words from Saturday echoed in her mind. It didn't sound like radical advice, but Meg was surprised how foreign the idea was. And coming from a priest, of all people. She wasn't sure what she'd expected. Maybe some solemnly-intoned Bible verses. Looking back on it, he'd hardly spoken at all, but what he'd said was so enticing it was almost seductive.

Don't be so hard on yourself.

Could it really be that simple?

Chapter Two

"Have you gained more weight?" Helen asked Thursday morning when Meg arrived at the pregnancy center.

"Since Saturday?" Meg grinned. "I haven't checked."

"It sneaks up on you," Helen warned. "I gained fifty pounds with my first baby. The next two . . ."

Meg nodded and pretended to listen. She'd learned not to take offense. It amazed her how many questions, warnings, and pieces of advice she got, now that she'd gotten big enough for people to tell she was pregnant. It didn't matter if they'd never seen her before in her life. It came from all sides: neighbors, grocery checkers, people in line behind her at the post office. When you were pregnant, your body was public domain.

". . . and they had to use forceps to get him out." Meg wasn't sure how Helen had gotten from weight gain to forceps so quickly. As the Joshua Center's only full-time employee, Helen worked the front desk, and Meg always hoped the pregnant women and teens who came through the lobby weren't forced to wait long enough to hear any of Helen's horror stories. The woman could go on about prenatal agony in a perfectly cheerful tone of voice, oblivious to the panic she might create. She didn't mean any harm. With Helen, it was just habit.

Meg did her best to keep her own ears shut. She didn't want to dwell on that part of the process. Not just yet.

Instead, she resorted to the best strategy she'd found to get Helen onto another subject. Meg nodded at the framed photographs on the other woman's desk. "But now your babies have babies. Three beautiful grand-children."

"I know." Helen caressed an oval frame with one finger. It held a picture of a laughing baby girl with curls popping out of her head like blond corkscrews. One of Meg's own baby pictures had looked like that, and she wondered if Jimmy would sport the same curls. She rested a hand on her stomach and tried to let herself feel the excitement without the guilt. *Don't be so hard on yourself.*

The weight of guilt lifted, ever so slightly.

"She's a little cutie," Helen said. "Still won't sleep through the night, though. You'll be lucky if you get any sleep the first six months after your baby's born. My daughter says she was teething again the other night . . ."

Meg switched her mental filter back on as she got ready to go to lunch.

Yes, she definitely felt better since her talk with the priest, although she suspected it was cheating. She hadn't really gone to confession for purification, at least not in the normally accepted sense. She'd gone so she could admit it, at least to herself—to unload. Maybe the two things weren't as different as they seemed.

Mojave Burger could use a major overhaul, Craig thought.

The little hamburger joint, in the heart of downtown Victory, had been built in the fifties or early sixties. He doubted they'd replaced the flooring in all that time. The huge black-and-white linoleum squares must have looked great when they were new, but they'd been dulled by years of foot traffic. Every time he came in here, he thought about talking to the owner about doing a face lift on the place. Keep the old-style look. Just make it new again. That was Craig's stock in trade.

But he had his hands full with the jobs he was juggling now. And the restaurant's tired look sure wasn't keeping any customers away. The food was too good. Mojave Burger proudly held its own against the tide of fast food chains that had been flooding the once-small town since Craig was in junior high. He was sure the burgers they served now were no more low-fat or health-conscious than the ones they'd served back in the sixties, but that was a huge part of the appeal. He ate here often these days, when he wasn't too grubby from working on the old church a few blocks away.

He was taking another bite of his double cheeseburger, savoring every calorie, when he saw a dark-haired woman in a flame-red jacket.

She stood near the front of the line, her back to him. There were two people behind her, but the bright red of her jacket called out to him from clear across the room.

It couldn't be. Could it? It was possible, he supposed. They were very close to the church where he'd accidentally heard that confession last Saturday. She probably lived or worked around here, like him.

On the other hand, there had to be lots of women in town with red jackets. He just had his pregnant confessor on the brain. Try as he might, he couldn't shake the nagging feeling that he'd done something rotten. It was like he'd opened her mail, or listened in over her telephone extension. If only he'd managed to speak up before her dirty laundry came spilling out.

As the woman ordered at the register, Craig tried not to stare. He knew things about her he had no business knowing—if it was the same woman. Seeing her from the back, he couldn't even tell if she was pregnant. Although the slim, shapely legs looked like the ones he remembered.

She finished ordering and moved down the side of the counter to wait for her food. She was pregnant, all right. Her stomach swelled out in front of her, almost out of context, like a room addition stuck onto the front lawn of a house. Craig studied her profile, trying to decide if it looked like the face of a woman who'd bared her soul a few days ago. She wore a contemplative expression as she gazed out the restaurant's double glass doors. Pretty—in a wholesome, maternal sort of way, of course. But she didn't look overwrought or tragic. She looked a lot like someone waiting for a burger.

The woman leaned against the counter and raised first one foot, then the other, as if to give each one a break from the weight they were supporting. The movement struck him as oddly graceful, and Craig reminded himself he'd been trying not to stare.

He turned his attention to the tabletop in front of him, where the gold sparkle imbedded in its surface was wearing away. *Really should talk to the owner,* he thought. Maybe after he'd finished the job on the church—

He glanced up again. She was headed his way with her tray, her eyes casting over the restaurant's limited number of tables. Craig knew what she was up against. An empty table at Mojave Burger in the middle of lunch hour—well, it wasn't impossible, but it took a lot of luck.

The restaurant crowd chatted on, oblivious to a pregnant woman's need for a table.

That was just wrong.

Craig rose to his feet.

Meg craned her neck, trying to see the row of booths on the other side of the room, when a man stood up in front of her. She stopped so quickly that her milk shake slid forward on her tray.

Tall. Substantially taller than she was, with broad shoulders hugged by a burgundy sweatshirt. That was all she could see at eye level. She moved her eyes upward over a firm chin, a bemused smile, and finally, dark blue eyes. They were smiling too.

Dark blue eyes, paired with nearly-black hair. It was a striking combination.

Inside her stomach, Jimmy did a flip, reacting to her sped-up heartbeat.

Thank goodness for Jimmy. His little somersault reminded her where she was, who she was, and how pregnant she was. "Excuse me." Meg tried to edge past her all-too-masculine obstacle.

"No, wait." The man gestured toward the booth beside him. "You can have this one."

She looked down at the table. There was still half a cheeseburger on his tray. "No, thanks. You're not finished."

"It's okay. I'm almost done."

"No, I'm fine." She tried to look past him for an open table. It was hard to see beyond those broad shoulders, but the prospects didn't appear to be getting any better. No one at the other tables looked ready to budge.

"Share?" His voice pulled her back to those deep blue eyes, ringed by an even deeper blue around the outside. He nodded at the worn padded vinyl of the empty seat across from him. "I promise I'll be out of your hair in a couple of minutes."

Meg wavered. He didn't look psychotic or homicidal. Far from it. And he wouldn't be trying to pick up on her, not in her condition.

"That's awfully nice of you," Meg hedged. She hesitated one moment more. Her ankles were starting to get that throbbing, puffy feeling that came when she stood for too long. Decision made, she dropped into the waiting seat. "Thanks."

Jimmy flipped over inside her again. Meg tried to concentrate on the baby's busy movements instead of the oh-so-solid frame of the man sitting back down in front of her. The sleeves of his sweatshirt were pushed up, revealing strong-looking forearms. The day was chilly—winter in Victory brought colder, nastier winds than Meg had expected when she moved to Southern California—but she had a feeling he kept the chill off by sheer activity. Everything about him looked and felt physical, in a very appealing way.

What was wrong with her? She had no business thinking about him that way. In the past several months, the opposite sex had been the farthest thing from her mind, and she wanted to keep it that way. Meg reached for her sandwich.

Craig tried to keep his eyes on his own food, but curiosity gnawed at him. He tried to ignore it. He'd already done his good deed for the day. Better to keep his mouth shut—and not take the chance that she might recognize his voice. Even if she was the woman from the confessional, what on earth was he supposed to do about it?

Finally, he caved in. "How many months . . . ?" he fumbled, nodding toward her pregnant midriff beneath the table.

"Seven." *When did Ron Reilly die?* Smiling, she reached below the table to touch her rounded stomach. "I know. You wouldn't think I could get any bigger."

Her smile surprised him. It brought a warmth to her expression that made her even prettier. Maybe this was that pregnant glow people always talked about. She certainly didn't look overburdened, or unhappy about the baby. The woman he'd talked to Saturday afternoon had sounded so distraught.

Craig watched as she peeled back the white wrapper of her sandwich, with "CX" for "chicken" scrawled across the top. On her left hand, she wore a wedding band. But then, he thought the woman he'd talked to probably would wear her ring, if only to keep up appearances.

Leave it alone, a part of him said. Another part of him had to know if she was the same woman.

Just as she parted her lips to take her first bite, he said, "You know, you're breaking an unwritten law."

Too late. Her mouth had sunk into the sandwich. Unable to reply, she looked at him quizzically over the bun.

Craig went on, "Nobody comes to Mojave Burger for

the grilled chicken sandwich. I think they only put them on the menu to keep the American Heart Association off their backs. This place is all about the double cheeseburgers."

She chewed her bite, and he waited for her to tell him to mind his own business. Which he probably should. If this was the right woman, he'd already heard things she'd never meant some non-ordained stranger to hear. Why get in any deeper?

She swallowed and hefted the sandwich slightly. "I'm watching my diet. For the baby." She rested a hand on her stomach once again. "But I'm hoping I can keep up a few good habits after the baby's born."

Craig considered his diminishing cheeseburger. "Oh, I don't know. I read an article once. It said if you exercise, stay away from fat and sugar, do all those healthy things, you know how much your life expectancy goes up? About six months."

He winced. If she was a widow, he probably shouldn't be kidding around about life expectancy. Trying to keep it light, he added, "What about that shake of yours? New kind of health food?"

She grinned. "Protein. Dairy products. They use real ice cream. I asked."

Her eyes glimmered with genuine humor. They were dark brown, a perfect match for the waves of hair tumbling around her face. And the soft curve of her up-turned mouth—

What was he thinking? The woman was pregnant. Very pregnant. But with the table between them obscuring her lower half, somehow it was easy to forget.

She didn't act like someone who'd been saddled with a baby to raise alone. Or someone hiding the secret of a loveless marriage. There must be some other pretty, dark-haired, pregnant woman in town.

But still, he wanted to know for sure. Craig searched for more small talk. "Do you work around here?"

"Not exactly. I just came from the Joshua Center. Ever heard of it?"

Craig frowned. "The pregnancy center, right?"

She nodded. "Best thing I ever did."

Craig felt disillusioned and he couldn't say why. So what if she went somewhere for help? If she was on her own, she probably needed all the help she could get. He'd just figured her for more self-reliant. Based on what, he couldn't say. "Isn't it for teenage girls?"

"Mostly. But there's no age limit." There was a new light in her eyes, an enthusiasm that puzzled him. "The thing is, we don't just refer them for social services. The idea is to get them counseling and job training, so they can support themselves. It's a real bootstraps mentality. I'm not a professional counselor, I just help around the office. And there's one girl I'm mentoring—"

Craig blinked, catching up. "You work there?"

"Well, volunteer. Only two days a week, and on Thursdays it's just in the morning. That's the day I'm on the night shift at my regular job."

Working for free, on top of a regular job? "Only" two days a week, while she was pregnant out to here? Not only was she not taking handouts, the woman was practically Joan of Arc.

At the mention of her regular job, her tone had changed. Her eyes, so enthusiastic a moment before, took on a shielded look. She must have realized she was giving a lot of personal information to someone she didn't really know.

He'd taken this as far as he ought to. And he'd finished his food. Definitely his cue to make an exit. Craig stood. "Well, I'd better get back to work myself." Inspiration struck. Grabbing a napkin, he wiped his right hand free of Mojave Burger's Secret Sauce and held it out to her. "Craig Stovall. Stovall Construction." He didn't usually throw the business name around, but it might help reassure her that he was on the level. And it might prompt her to give her own name in return. Her name would tell him, once and for all, if she was Ron Reilly's widow.

She accepted his hand, her fingers warm and slender, her eyes still wary. "I'm Megan." She left off her last name and he knew it wasn't an accident.

Leave well enough alone, he told himself again. Craig let go of her hand with a strange reluctance.

"Thanks for the table," she said belatedly as he turned away.

He turned back, and there it was again. That smile, with that same sparkle, had returned. "I owe you one," she said.

"Forget it." He didn't want her to forget it, any more than he wanted to leave without finding out her name. And in that moment, looking at that radiant smile, he wasn't sure if Ron Reilly or secret confessions had a thing to do with it.

"Have a nice day," he said lamely.

As he backed away, he nearly stumbled into an elderly couple as they got up to leave their table.

"So, how's the baby?"

Meg crossed the tiny break room at the Joshua Center, a trip which required very few steps, and handed the pregnant teen a cup of hot chocolate.

Jackie accepted the cup from Meg with a wry grin. "Huge."

There was no disputing that. Jackie bore eight months worth of pregnancy on her tiny frame. The break room's oversized couch practically swallowed the rest of her, but her stomach bulged in front, the perfect resting place for a styrofoam cup of instant cocoa.

Meg eased into the armchair alongside the couch with her own cup. "Don't feel bad. It's nice to be around someone who's more pregnant than me."

They both laughed, but a hint of awkwardness hung in the air. Meg could tell there was something on Jackie's mind. They'd been meeting here every Saturday for the past five months, but even if they hadn't been, Jackie wasn't hard to read.

She didn't beat around the bush, either. "You think I

should give the baby up for adoption, don't you?" Jackie blurted.

"I can't answer that question for you." Meg had her own opinions, but under the Center's policies, she had to keep them to herself. "That's something you have to decide for yourself."

"You think I should give it up," Jackie repeated. Her gray eyes didn't waver. For someone who'd made some foolish choices, Jackie had surprising strengths. One of them was her ability to make direct eye contact without flinching, even when she was talking about a difficult subject.

"You're keeping yours," Jackie added, almost accusingly.

Meg had never heard that note of resentment in Jackie's voice before, but she knew better than to take it personally. The girl was a month away from her due date, with her boyfriend long since out of the picture. She'd grown up without a father, and her mother's chief reaction to the pregnancy had been annoyance at the prospect of having another mouth to feed. Jackie had a lot to deal with. And not all of it was her own doing.

Meg said, "I can't say what I'd do in your shoes."

"You *are* in my shoes."

"Not exactly."

"Because you were married." The accusing tone was back.

"There's more to it than that. I'm older. I've got more job experience." Meg kept her eyes on Jackie's, meeting the girl's challenge. "I'm done with high school."

That had been a near thing, but Jackie didn't need to know that. When Meg's parents had died in a car crash during her senior year, she'd been on her own almost as suddenly as Jackie. But she'd only been responsible for herself. Not a baby.

Soon she would be. Maybe she and Jackie weren't so different after all. It was one of the reasons she volunteered at the Joshua Center. It was ironic, finding she had more in common with an unwed pregnant sixteen-year-old than with the high school graduates she supervised at the store on a daily basis. Meg reminded herself, as she'd just reminded Jackie, that she was better equipped to raise a child on her own—at least, a little.

Jackie was silent, and for the first time, her steady gaze wavered. Meg pressed her advantage. "You're right," she said, more gently. "I *was* married. And things still didn't work out the way I planned. Even when we start off with the best odds, things can happen that we don't have any control over. We just have to make the best choices we can."

Jackie bit her lip, and Meg bit her tongue. Bright as the girl was, Meg still couldn't see her raising a baby on her own. But it wasn't her place to say so.

"I guess what I wanted was to have a real family," Jackie said. Her eyes were red-rimmed, but she didn't cry.

Meg found room to be grateful. She hadn't had her parents long enough, but they'd loved her.

"We all want that," Meg said. Her next words came from the bottom of her heart. "But you can't count on someone else being there to take care of you. I guess we both learned that the hard way."

Jackie lowered her eyes. "I'm sorry your husband died. My boyfriend was just a jerk."

Meg could have echoed that, but it wouldn't help. "Nobody's perfect."

"Your husband wouldn't have run out on you."

Would he have? Meg wondered. She'd never know for sure.

But it was a question she asked herself every day. Most days, she decided Ron would have borne it with a stiff upper lip, the same way he had when he let her take the part-time job at Rosie's Rags. The job that had just about saved her life when she found herself alone again. Twice in her life she'd had her support yanked out from under her. It wasn't going to happen again. If she'd learned one lesson, that was it.

Of all the blasted clichés, Ron had been big and strong. After years of taking care of herself, that had looked pretty good to Meg. Later on, she'd become aware of the domineering, the possessiveness, the need to have her at his beck and call.

And being big and strong was no help at all when your plane dropped out of the sky.

Meg shifted in her chair, only partly to find a better position. "We're supposed to talk about your school work," she said, and Jackie smiled with visible relief as they returned to more comfortable ground.

After Jackie left, Meg went into the back office and started on the filing. She hadn't gotten very far when Helen walked in. "There's a man up front to see you." Behind her glasses, she studied Meg with undisguised curiosity.

Meg slid the file drawer slowly shut as a feeling of premonition washed over her. It wasn't as if she hung around with a lot of men these days.

Sure enough, when she rounded the corner into the main lobby, Craig Stovall waited, big as life and handsomer than she remembered. Not that she'd been thinking about him. Much.

He stood at the other side of the front desk, his deep blue eyes evident from twenty paces away. It must be the dark blue color of the sweater he wore today. Meg stopped short and had a flashback. She could almost hear her shake sliding forward on her tray.

Her guard went up. A stalker, that's what he was. She should have known better. What in the world had she been thinking when she met him at the burger place last week? She'd chatted happily away, until she suddenly remembered she didn't know him from Adam. Had she forgotten that much about a single woman's safety in less than two years of marriage? Now, here was the result. Here he was, to. . . . to what?

"Helen told me you accept donations here," he said.

He'd already learned Helen's name. Fast worker. "That's right." Meg took a cautious step forward.

He rested a hand on the desk in front of him, shifting his weight awkwardly. If she hadn't been smarter, Meg would have found something endearing in that awkwardness, or in the way his thick, dark hair fell loosely across his forehead. He looked anything but menacing. Conscious of Helen's stare, Meg put on a smile. "Do you have something for us?"

"A rocking chair. It's out in my truck."

So that was it. He planned to get her out of the building and drag her screaming into his truck, never to be seen again.

Okay, so that was pretty unlikely. That didn't mean she was foolish enough to take the chance. Meg looked dubiously past Craig to the lobby's glass door, with First Street just beyond it. "Can you bring it in?"

He gave a loose shrug, and Meg couldn't help noticing the movement of his broad shoulders underneath the turtleneck.

A moment later he returned, carrying a wooden rocker upside down over his shoulder. Belatedly, Meg went to hold the door, but he'd already ducked inside. With surprisingly fluid movement, he managed to avoid hitting the chair against either the top or the side of the doorway. Once inside, he eased the chair right side up and onto the floor, and Meg drew in her breath.

The dark wood of the rocker gleamed like new. Meg caught a faint, nutty scent of varnish. Craig rested one hand on the back of the chair, sliding his fingers over its polished surface with an air of quiet pride.

Meg looked up for Helen's reaction, but uncharacteristically, the woman had made herself scarce.

Meg dropped her guard enough to step forward and finger one of the rocker's tapered arms. Something about the shiny smoothness of the wood begged to be touched. "It's beautiful," she said. "Where did it come from?"

"Well, to be honest, it turned up in the attic of a house I'm working on." Craig looked down at the chair. "It seemed like a shame to let it go to waste."

He hadn't found it in an attic looking like this. "You've done some work on it."

That big, loose shrug again. "A little." He ran his fingers between the slim vertical rungs of the chair, and Meg found herself staring at the contrast between the rough hand and the delicately knobbed poles of wood. Meg fingered one of the intricate rungs. Smooth and glossy, with no trace of splinters. It would be a perfect chair for rocking a baby. Add a cushion for the seat, maybe in a gingham or floral fabric. But not for the back. It would be a shame to hide those beautifully shaped rungs.

Not the work of a stalker, she thought.

Meg realized she was picturing it in the baby's room

of her own apartment. But no. She could find someone else who needed it more, someone who was really having trouble getting furniture for her baby.

"Are you sure you want to give this up?" she said. "Isn't it an antique?"

He gave a short spurt of laughter. "Well, I guess anything from the nineteen fifties qualifies as an antique by now. But it's nothing special. You should have seen it when I found it."

Meg glanced at him quizzically, but his eyes shifted away. "I mean, the wood was nothing to write home about. Just a cheap maple. But that's the great thing about wood. Unless it's particle board or something like that, you can work with it. Find the grain. Bring out the beauty in it." His fingers trailed absently over the slender slats, bumping into hers briefly. Both of them pulled their hands back quickly, and Meg's mouth went dry.

Big and strong, Meg warned herself. But there was something surprisingly gentle about the way his fingers had caressed the rich, dark wood. She smiled. "Well, you did a beautiful job. You must have spent a lot of time on it."

He had, but Craig didn't want her to know that. He lowered his gaze once more, away from her perceptive-looking dark eyes. "It was no big deal," he said. "I like to keep busy."

"The devil makes work for idle hands," she said.

He should have known. She was a religious fanatic.

Although in Craig's case, the saying was more true than she knew.

But her tone was light, and when he glanced at her face, he saw a playful smile there. He didn't see how anyone could help smiling back.

What was he doing here, anyway? He'd become determined to find out once and for all whether she was the woman he'd talked to in the confessional.

"So, do you think someone could use it?" That wasn't what he wanted to say. He made a living working with his hands, but he thought of himself as a pretty bright guy. Why was he at a loss for words? He couldn't think of a simple way to find out who she was. *So, what's your last name? Didn't you used to be married to that dead guy?* No way.

"Absolutely," Meg said. It took him a minute to remember the question he'd just asked. "If you're sure you want to give it up." The playful light was back in her eyes. "Maybe you'd like to hang on to it for your own baby."

"Uh, no." He felt his face go red. "No plans on that right now."

Meg bit her lip, and he saw her blush, too, as if she'd said something she hadn't meant to. Suddenly, her dark eyes focused everywhere but on him.

"Well, I'd better get going." Craig backed toward the exit and pulled when he should have pushed; the door rattled in its frame. Just before he escaped, he looked back at her one more time. Pretty as ever, and looking more than a little puzzled. "Good luck with your baby," he said, just as he scooted out.

As if his well wishes would do her any good at all.

Meg watched through the glass door as Craig clambered into a blue pickup truck. She couldn't hold back a smile. His exit hadn't been nearly as graceful as his entrance. Maybe that was what happened to all men when the subject of a baby came up.

What was with her? Pregnancy hormones? One minute she'd vowed to use common sense, to be more careful. The next minute she was practically flirting with the guy. Or what passed for flirting in her limited experience, anyway. Flirting, when she was seven months pregnant and as big as a house. If it hadn't been so pitiful, Meg would have laughed out loud.

But it *was* a beautiful chair. Meg fingered the rungs again, tracing the minute curves and swells where Craig's hands had been.

Helen reappeared, and Meg followed the older woman's gaze through the glass door. Outside, the truck sat poised, waiting for a gap in the First Street traffic to pull out of its curbside parking space. The cab's roof shadowed Craig's profile. "That's Jan Stovall's boy," Helen said.

"Boy" wasn't the word that came to mind. "You know him?"

"Since he was about seven," Helen said. "He lived down the street from me until he grew up and moved out. Got into a lot of trouble back when he was in high school." Meg's ears pricked up. Resolutely, she kept from turning her head. "Then he started that construction business," Helen went on. "He's fixed up a lot of buildings in this part of town."

Meg braced herself for the other shoe to drop. With Helen, there was bound to be more. *But they say he roams the streets at night, lurking outside the bedroom windows of innocent women. . . .*

Meg glanced at the other woman expectantly. Helen watched Craig pull away, as if he might overhear, before she made her final pronouncement:

"He's really turned himself around."

Chapter Three

Megan bit into her chicken sandwich and found her eyes wandering to the entrance of Mojave Burger. When she caught herself, she pulled her gaze away.

It wasn't as if she expected to bump into Craig here again. What were the odds? No, she'd simply discovered a place that happened to make a halfway-decent grilled chicken sandwich. Even if it was a little farther from the clothing store than she liked to go on her lunch break. Even if it was her second chicken sandwich in less than a week, since the day Craig had dropped by the pregnancy center with his surprise donation. Grilled chicken must be her first official pregnancy craving.

At any rate, she had more important things on her mind. Like getting Jimmy's nursery stocked and ready before he arrived. She went over her mental checklist yet again. She'd been shopping systematically at bargain and thrift stores for the last several months, spreading out the expenses so they wouldn't hit her all at once. The insurance and military benefits following Ron's death had left her a little safety net, but she'd needed some of that money to move out of the Air Force base housing. She had no intention of disturbing her nest egg again unless she absolutely had to. She didn't want to be caught short in a genuine emergency just because she'd blown all her savings on pacifiers.

She had enough newborn-sized clothing, and a few outfits for when Jimmy grew out of those. And an old dresser, which Meg had repainted, to put them in. Colorful wrist rattles. Bottles . . . blankets . . . a bassinet . . . It was a lot like shopping for Christmas, and waiting for the big day when she could give the baby all his presents.

A sweatshirted figure walked into the restaurant, and Meg's head went up. She hadn't even been aware she was watching the door again.

And the short, gray-haired man who walked in wasn't Craig Stovall. Not even close. Meg felt her heart race and realized she was behaving like a schoolgirl.

Chicken sandwich craving, indeed.

The last thing she wanted was a man in her life. She knew where that had gotten her the last time. Cooped up, dependent, and all but helpless when he was so abruptly gone. She'd vowed never to need anyone again, and here she was, eating at a place she wouldn't ordinarily go—not this often, anyway—and pretending it was just for the food.

This wouldn't do. Meg told herself the gray-haired man was a wake-up call.

She'd come here for the wrong reasons, but it wasn't too late to correct her mistake before she made a fool of herself. She wasn't going to catch Craig here, and Craig wasn't going to catch her acting like a high-school freshman. Meg dug into her meal with a vengeance, resolving to finish fast and get out of here. From now on, if she really wanted lunch from Mojave Burger, she could drive through.

She had one bite of her sandwich left when the real Craig Stovall strolled in, his eyes skimming the room, rather than aiming straight toward the counter. He picked her out, and Meg felt as if she'd been pinned to the spot. Those blue eyes were impossible to miss, even from halfway across the restaurant.

A casual grin, a nod, and he sauntered to the counter to order.

Meg felt her face burn like a four-alarm fire. Oh no. She wasn't going to be trapped by her own stupidity. She didn't want involvement of any kind, even if her subconscious had lured her here under false pretenses. Freed from her blue-eye-induced paralysis now that Craig's back was turned, she had the chance to make her move. Straight out the door.

Meg seized her tray, dumped its contents into the nearest waste bin, and barreled toward the exit. Unfortunately, the exit was the same door as the entrance, and it took her within a few feet of Craig. *Just keep moving.*

She tried to slip out quickly, but when you were seven months pregnant, it was hard to move very fast, and harder still not to be noticed. Craig glanced at her again just as she passed; Meg flashed a too-wide, *sorry–gotta–go* smile at him and lunged out through the heavy glass door.

On her way to her car, she groped in her purse. Then deeper. Still no luck. She took the purse by the opposite ends of its strap and shook it, but she didn't hear the familiar metallic rattle. Her heart sank.

Her car keys weren't in it.

As Craig finished placing his order with the counter girl, a red-jacketed flurry swept back inside, just at the edge of his peripheral vision.

He turned to track the red blur and saw Megan flag down one of the ever-vigilant employees who was swabbing down tables. Moments later, the boy took the lid off a trash container and started sifting through its contents.

"Sir?" the counter girl prodded Craig. "Your change."

Craig took the money absent-mindedly and turned once again toward the mini-drama unfolding at the trash can. The acne-scarred kid was still searching through the mountain of slightly used double burgers. Megan was half-leaning over, trying to help. With her pregnant stomach in the way, it was an awkward pose, but it also accented her long, slim legs as she stood on tiptoe and poked through the trash.

Didn't pregnant women gain any weight in their

legs? And didn't she ever get cold wearing dresses in the winter?

Maybe it was those legs. Maybe he had an undiscovered thing for damsels in distress. Or maybe he just would have felt like a clod if he'd done anything else. Whatever it was, something pulled Craig in that direction. "What happened?"

Megan didn't look up. "I threw away my car keys," she said with obvious disgust. "At least I think so." Her movements were rigid, as if she'd been wound up tightly, and frustration came from her in palpable waves. Craig wondered if he was getting his first undisguised look at the harried pregnant widow from the confessional.

"Bad day?" he asked.

Her dark eyes met his, flashing with such exasperation that Craig was taken aback. In that moment, he could have sworn her frustration was directed at him. But that was ridiculous. She'd just lost her keys, he reminded himself; he simply happened to be standing in the wrong spot.

He moved toward the trash can to take her place, edging her out as he reached in to help the hapless burger jockey dig.

"It's okay. You don't have to. Really," she protested.

Craig saw no need to argue the point. He kept searching.

As gravity would have it, the keys turned up near the

bottom of the trash bag, swimming in someone else's ketchup and mustard. Craig hooked the round metal ring over his little finger, avoiding most of the sauce. "Be right back."

"Wait." Megan's voice was strained. "Where—"

"To rinse them off. Wait right here." He nodded a thanks to the burger jockey as the kid silently replaced the lid on the trash container.

"I—" Meg felt her face flush. All she wanted was to get away from him, from those blue eyes and that sympathetic attitude, before she said or did something stupid. Something *else* stupid, even stupider than dumping her keys in the trash. "I'm already late."

"You can't drive with these." He smiled at her, holding the gooey key ring aloft. Was he always so calm and reasonable? Meg fought the urge to soften under his laid-back grin. Especially when he was dangling her escape right in front of her eyes.

"Here." Craig pulled his cell phone from the belt of his jeans and put it into her hand. "You can call and say you're on the way. I'll be back in ten seconds."

"But—"

He wasn't listening. "I'll be right back," he repeated, and headed to the men's room.

Meg stared after Craig's retreating figure—maddeningly packaged in those faded denim jeans—and forced herself not to scream. Just what she didn't need. Another commandeering male, with that take-charge, accept–no–arguments attitude. He'd snatched matters completely out of her hands and left her to stand there, helpless. The big, strong ones were like that. The big, strong ones, who still managed to look and smell good, even when they worked with their hands all day.

The sooner she got out of here, the better. Except she couldn't get out of here, because he had her car keys.

Craig was drying the keys with a paper towel when he saw the insignia on the key chain. A small laurel wreath, circled around a gold star. So small he never would have seen it if he hadn't been rinsing her keys. But he knew what the little gold star meant. It was the insignia for family members of Air Force personnel who died in the line of duty. Growing up in a military town, you learned about things like that.

Now he knew for sure. She *was* a widow. Ron Reilly's widow.

Craig didn't know why that should make his heart drop into his stomach. He'd had a pretty good idea all along. But this made it real. This meant she was the woman from the confessional. New guilt surged through him, and he was surprised at the difference between wondering and knowing. She'd spilled her guts to him and she didn't even know it. He felt like he'd been caught pawing through her dresser drawers.

When he came out of the men's room, Megan stood right where he'd left her. She was glaring at him.

She knew what he'd done. She must know. Why else would she look at him like that? Suddenly her tense attitude made sense. Craig fumbled for words to explain, trying to remember just how he'd come to impersonate a priest.

It was too hard to continue meeting her eyes, so Craig lowered his eyes and found himself focusing on her mouth. That didn't help at all. She licked her lips, obviously agitated, and it gave Craig the most absurd idea in the world for a way to soothe that agitation. A way to make that now-firm line of her lips melt away. . . .

That was, if they weren't in the middle of a burger joint, if she wasn't pregnant, and if she didn't look halfway ready to shoot him down at ten paces.

She took the renegade keys from his hand. "Thanks. But you didn't need to do that." Her words were civil, but her tone held carefully controlled annoyance.

"I'm sorry. I—" Wait. Why was he apologizing? This wasn't about him being a phony priest, he realized. She was fussing about the car keys. Why should she be annoyed with him about that?

"I was trying to *help*," he said, annoyance creeping into his own voice. But if he'd learned one thing from his chaotic high school days, it was how to control his temper.

"I can take care of myself," she said. She quickly started past him toward the door, as if she were running away from something. Craig put a hand on her arm, and she swiveled around sharply. What was her problem?

Craig reminded her, "My cell phone?"

He half expected her to explode in a final tempest of female irrationality. Instead, her eyes wavered, and he thought he glimpsed a chink in whatever wall she'd thrown up around her. For the first time in the last ten minutes, Craig understood her reaction. The forgotten cell phone was one more lousy note in a lousy day.

She put the phone firmly into his hand, then turned away.

"Megan?" She stopped again. "Are you okay?" He didn't know what made him say it.

She didn't meet his eyes. In fact, her gaze darted everywhere else, as if casting around for an answer. When she looked at him again, her expression was urgent, and he couldn't tell if she was furious or desperate.

"Just—stop being nice to me," she said, then turned and left.

For the umpteenth time that afternoon, Meg fingered the telephone directory on its little shelf behind the counter at Rosie's Rags. There it was, right below the cash register. It would be easy enough to call Craig and apologize; just look in the Victory Yellow Pages under construction.

She never should have been so rude. She'd regretted it before she even started her car in the Mojave Burger parking lot, using her just-washed key in the ignition of her old Ford. Craig had helped her, and she'd all but bitten his head off. If she had it to do over again, she would have acted differently.

She should apologize. But talking to Craig again would only open a door she had a feeling was best left closed.

Yes, it was better this way.

Meg twirled the little countertop display case, with its assorted costume jewelry items. Anything to keep her hands off that phone book. At the other end of the store, Stephanie and Kim fastidiously refolded the jeans on their tabletop displays, talking quietly to each other. Meg had set them on the task when she got back from lunch. From their hushed tones and obedient attitude, she could tell they'd sensed her mood.

Meg sighed. This was her own fault. She knew all about the dangers of leaning on someone. Yet she'd gone back, more than once, to a place where she knew Craig was likely to show up sooner or later. She couldn't kid herself that she didn't know why, not any more. One look at a pair of blue eyes and broad shoulders, one friendly conversation, and she forgot her hard-learned lessons. As if a man in his undisputed prime would want anything to do with a single mother-to-be, anyway.

Yes, it was better if he thought she was just a jerk. If she'd wanted Craig out of her life, with all the temptations he represented, she'd done a good job.

Definitely for the best, Meg told herself. Again.

She could stand on her own two feet. And she could go back to brown-bagging her lunch. She should be saving the money anyway.

Meg glanced back over at Stephanie and Kim, huddled at the other end of the store as if it were a separate country. Immediately, she thought of a use for some of the extra pocket change she'd just picked up.

"Hey, guys," she called across the store. Both girls' heads snapped up, and Meg winced. When had she made the transformation from teenager to authority figure? But she was the boss now—the second-string boss, at least—and that wasn't going to change. That didn't mean she couldn't be a human being.

"Who wants a Coke?" Meg inclined her head toward the little convenience store two doors down. "You fly . . . I'll buy."

Meg slumped on the floor of the baby's future nursery and looked despairingly at the pieces of white-painted wood that littered the floor around her. Day two of her attempt to assemble Jimmy's diaper table, and she was ready to give up. It was the one piece of baby furniture she'd bought brand new, and it had beaten her. She'd tried phoning the discount store where she'd bought it, but they'd been no help at all.

She didn't know many people in Victory, but she knew one person who could fix her problem in a blink of an eye. And the last thing in the world she wanted to do was call him.

She wanted, with all her heart, to be able to take care of herself. Depending on other people got you worse than hurt. It left you helpless, and she was determined not to let it happen again. But in moments like this, there were definite drawbacks to being independent.

She patted Jimmy. "Don't worry, honey. I'll work it out."

Meg closed her eyes to shut out the sight of the scattered pieces and screws. Maybe it was time to think of a compromise.

"We've got to stop meeting like this."

Craig looked up from his Mojave Burger in time to see Megan Reilly drop unceremoniously into the seat across from him in the booth. Her smile was all sweetness and light, with no trace of the glares she'd flashed at him the other day. But Craig remembered. He'd learned his lesson. No point in sticking his nose where it wasn't wanted.

That smile alone probably would have melted most guys, but Craig didn't return it. Not yet. Not after the other day. The other day had shown him it didn't always pay to offer help where it wasn't asked for, or even wanted. His strange little crusade had ended there.

Craig looked at her warily and waited. Megan drew in a visible breath and spoke again without preamble. "Craig, I was rude the other day and I'm sorry." She raked her fingers through her hair; it sent lush, dark waves tumbling back down around her face. He tried not to imagine how it would feel to slide his own fingers through that silky-looking hair.

Pregnant out to here, Craig reminded himself, and swallowed hard.

He waited for her to say more, but apparently there wasn't any. Usually an apology was followed by some sort of excuse or explanation. When Megan didn't offer any, he found himself supplying one. "You were stressed."

Helping her again, he realized. But just so she could unload her conscience and be done with it.

"Maybe," Megan said. "But that's no excuse. You did me a favor, and I acted like a jerk."

He let the smile come. It didn't cost him anything, he reasoned. "Forget it."

Instead of relaxing, she shifted against the faded red vinyl of the booth. If anything, she looked more uncomfortable. Craig relented a little further. "So are you here for lunch?"

Her smile faded. "No, I can't stay. I—have a proposition."

Craig leaned back a little, wary again, wondering where this was going. "Not every day I get propositioned by a pregnant woman."

She reddened. Craig squirmed. He shouldn't have said that. But why should he make it easy for her? He'd already gone too far out of his way, and for no good reason—widow or not, confession or not.

Megan took a deep breath, and her blush faded a little. "I'm not very good at accepting help from people.

That's why I acted the way I did. But I could really use a favor. If you'll let me pay you back." She took another deep breath, and Craig wondered what in the world was coming. "Do you like chocolate cake?"

Craig blinked. Stranger and stranger. Biting back another smile, he said, "I'm diabetic."

"Oh." As Craig studied her, blue eyes inscrutable, Meg felt heat in her cheeks once again. Diabetic? She hadn't thought of anything like that. Her mind scrambled for an alternative. "How about . . ."

She eyed the tall wax paper cup in front of Craig and stopped. "You are not." By now she could recognize one of Mojave Burger's milk shakes as well as anyone; the cactus plants smattered on the sides of the cup were red, rather than green like the ones on the soda cups.

Craig's face broke out in a grin, and she forced herself not to smile back. He wasn't making this easy. Which was obviously the point.

Craig rested an arm against the back of the booth, as if he were settling back to enjoy a really good movie. "How about if you tell me what you want, and I'll name my price." It was a questionable choice of words, and he seemed to realize it. The teasing grin faded. "Seriously," he said. "Just tell me what it is."

This was harder than she'd expected. Meg ran a hand through her hair again and lowered her eyes. "I've had a half-assembled diaper table on the floor in my apartment for days now. I'm stuck. Is there any way . . ." She floundered, studying the tabletop. It had faded flecks of gold. She'd never noticed that before.

"That's it?"

Craig's voice brought her head back up. The blue eyes were no longer cool or teasing. They were staring at her in honest astonishment. "Megan, that's *nothing*. You don't have to pay me back for that."

The grin stole over his face again, and this time Meg couldn't stop herself from returning it. "But I never say no to chocolate cake."

Chapter Four

Craig checked the label on the gray metal mailbox with Megan's apartment number. *M. REILLY.* Her last name removed any lingering doubt about who she was, or who her husband had been. He'd better stay on his toes, or he'd say something wrong and reveal himself as a priest impersonator yet.

Better finish this job quick.

Craig walked through the open courtyard, found the door with the right number, and knocked. The complex wasn't gated in any way. If she was living by herself, she really should find a safer place.

Then she opened the door, and all thoughts of home security deserted him.

Was he developing a thing for pregnant women? Her long, butter-yellow sweater skimmed past her rounded middle and left off part way down her thighs. She wore slim, dark brown slacks and flat black shoes, the kind a dancer might wear. She looked soft and relaxed, a woman at home on a Sunday morning, and the scent of chocolate cake that wafted out over the threshold threatened to undo him.

It didn't occur to Craig until the intoxicating scent reached him that she might be auditioning him for husband number two. One more thing to watch out for. If the cake tasted as good as it smelled, he could see some poor sucker falling for it. But not him.

Megan stepped back. "Come on in."

Step into my parlor? No, he was getting paranoid. He went inside, somehow expecting the inside of the apartment to be as warm and inviting as the sweater and the smell of chocolate. But no. The small living room had an oddly generic look—couch, coffee table, television set, bookshelf. No pictures on the walls; no photos anywhere that he could see. Skimming the bookshelf for titles, he glimpsed *The Power of a Praying Woman, What to Expect When You're Expecting,* and several Dean Koontz thrillers.

"The nursery is this way." She beckoned slightly with her head as she turned to lead him down a short hallway and into a tiny room to the left.

Tiny, yes. But it only took a glance to see where Megan's heart was in this apartment. A big, used-looking armchair sat near the window, a blue and yellow knit afghan thrown casually over it. Next to the chair was a dresser with farm animal characters for knobs; on top of it sat a lamp with a purple cow and a bright pink pig at its base. Like every room in every apartment Craig had ever seen, including his own, the walls were white, but a wallpaper border ringed the room at eye level, with comical barnyard animals frolicking on a grass-green background. The whole room exuded brightness and cheer.

Except for the middle of the floor, which held the obvious source of frustration: a partially assembled piece of white wooden furniture, along with pliers, a screwdriver, and a crumpled set of directions.

"I hope I didn't screw it up too much." Megan sounded more hesitant than she had in the restaurant.

"Oh, I doubt it." Craig settled down with his box of tools. Here, at least, was something he could fix. Unlike the problems of a woman fending for herself without a husband, or a baby growing up without a father.

Meg hovered in the doorway as Craig crouched, frowned, and began sizing up what had begun to remind her of a white wooden carcass. After a moment, he opened his toolbox and reached for a screwdriver.

She ventured, "Don't you want to look at the instructions first?"

He glanced up and fixed her with an amused smile that made her pulse skitter ahead. "Oh, I don't think so."

That was a man for you. Meg took a step back. "I'll go check on the cake," she said, and made her retreat.

Inside the kitchen, she wiped her damp palms against the sides of her sweater. She already knew how the cake was doing; she'd taken it out of the oven fifteen minutes ago. It would be some time before it was cool enough for the icing.

Meg spent a few minutes uselessly pacing around the small island that took up most of the floor space in her kitchen. Why was she so nervous? She was hiding in her own home. This was crazy, the very sort of reaction she'd resolved to avoid. He was doing her a favor, and she was baking him a cake. *Quid pro quo.* No expectations, no strings on either side.

And she had at least twenty minutes to kill before she could frost the cake.

Meg decided she was being not only ridiculous, but rude. Squaring her shoulders, she went back to the nursery to see how the diaper table was faring.

The carcass still lay on its side, but it already bore a stronger resemblance to what it was meant to be. With his dark head bent over the task, Craig seemed unaware of her reappearance. Meg took the moment to watch his ease as he lined up another shelf with one of the supporting side rails and began twisting a screw in with no wasted motion. It looked so simple when he did it. Meg tried not to feel like an ignoramus.

"Can I get you anything?" she asked.

"No, thanks," he said without looking up. The beige down vest he'd been wearing when he arrived lay in an ungainly heap behind him. She should hang it up. But Craig and the diaper table were between Meg and the vest. Still uncertain what to do, she sank to the floor just inside the doorway, tucking her legs under her. It didn't seem polite to abandon him again like some kind of a hired work crew.

"I found your problem," Craig said. "Your big mistake was trusting those directions. They'd screw anyone up."

"Oh? I thought you didn't need the instructions."

He grinned. "Well, I had to look, to see how you ended up where you did. They left out a whole diagram. This part—" he tapped at one of the painted white supports "—can't go in, until you've got this other one in place."

Meg felt a small rush of vindication. So she wasn't so incompetent after all.

After a few moments of silence, Craig glanced up—not at her, but at the wall. "Nice room," he said. "But isn't the landlord going to give you heck about the wallpaper?"

Meg shook her head. "It's a temporary border. It peels right off." She felt Jimmy shift as he adjusted to their new position on the floor. She put a hand to that side of her stomach and tried to guess what she was feeling. An elbow? A foot?

Craig continued to look around the room as he worked. "There's no crib in here," he noted.

"I won't need one right away," Meg said. "Newborn babies wake up a lot at night, so I've got a bassinet set up by the side of the bed."

Craig grimaced. "That sounds brutal." He looked at her for the first time since she'd come back into the room. "I mean—it's just you by yourself, right?"

She should have known it would come up eventually. Meg studied the bland gray carpet. "My husband died in a plane crash six months ago." This was the part where people offered their condolences, and she never knew what to say after that. She'd taken to settling for a small smile and a demure "thank you," like some sort of humble Academy Award winner.

"I know," he said. She raised her head in surprise; Craig's eyes were down again as he twisted another screw into place. "I saw your name on the mailbox. You were married to Ron Reilly, right?"

"Right." She tried to see his face, but he seemed very intent on this particular screw.

"I knew him, a little," he said.

"You did?"

"We went to the same high school." Craig searched the carpet around his knees until he picked up a stray bolt. "It's not like we hung out together or anything. He was a year ahead of me, for one. And you know how it is in high school. Everybody's got their own niche."

She already knew what Ron's was. He'd been the football quarterback. Craig looked fairly athletic, too. "So what was your niche?" she asked.

He glanced up long enough to give her a crooked

grin. "Troublemaker." Once again, his eyes shifted back to the table. It looked nearly done. "But don't worry, I gave it up a long time ago."

I know. She almost quoted his line back at him, but maybe he wouldn't appreciate Helen talking about his checkered past. "What kind of trouble?"

"Teenage kid stuff, mostly. A few curfew violations, a little reckless driving . . ." He trailed off, his eyes wandering restlessly over his project, the floor, the walls, before they settled on her again. His brow furrowed. "Are you okay?" he asked.

"What?" Puzzled, Meg followed his glance to her hand, where it still rested on her stomach. It had become such second nature, she didn't even realize she was doing it. "Oh. No. The baby's fine. I just like to feel him move around."

"What's it feel like?" He frowned. "Indigestion?"

She laughed. "No, it's not like something I ate." Craig reddened; it felt good to have a turn making him blush. "It's more like—well, like there's someone in there." She smoothed her hand over her sweater. "It's funny. I know this is just a tiny part of the time I'll have him. But he's already such a big part of my life."

His gaze lingered on her face. "You're really excited about this baby, aren't you?"

He seemed so perplexed. "Of course."

"It just doesn't sound like much fun, raising a kid all by yourself."

She lifted her chin. "It wasn't my idea." The truth

was, she'd been wondering when someone was going to come out and say it. Single motherhood was more widely accepted these days, but the question was still there, under the surface. Meg could understand. Raising a baby alone wouldn't be easy—but she'd never wanted anything in her life as much as she wanted Jimmy.

"Sorry." Craig inclined his head slightly. "So why in the world are you volunteering at a crisis pregnancy center right now? Seems like you've got enough problems as it is."

Now, *that* was a question she hadn't expected. She tried to think of an explanation simpler than the truth, but she couldn't. Meg took a deep breath. "Do you believe in God?"

"Sure." His expression was cautious, but his answer reassured her. She wondered why it mattered so much.

"Well, when Ron died and I found out I was pregnant, I felt pretty sorry for myself for a while there. So I prayed about it." She lowered her eyes. "It's not like I go around expecting God to talk to me personally. I figure he's got more important things to do. But these words came into my head, clear as a bell: 'Find someone who's worse off than you are.'" She looked deeper into the carpet fibers, embarrassed. "I don't mean I heard a voice or anything. And probably it was just me, thinking. But it made sense. And it was a good idea. It helped me get my mind off myself."

Craig was silent for so long, she finally had to sneak a peek back up at him. He was staring at her, making no pretense at doing anything else. His gaze felt heavy, examining her until she felt strangely exposed. It was like a direct hit to her solar plexus. This late in the pregnancy, she wouldn't have thought she remembered where her solar plexus was. She gripped a few threads of the carpet, as if they could steady her.

At last he broke the silence. "Do you have any family out here? Anyone to give you a hand?"

"No." She didn't really want to go into her hard luck story about being an orphan alone in California. But he continued to study her, as if waiting for more. And though Meg couldn't read his eyes, she felt as if they could see right into her. Couldn't he go back to studying the floor, or the wallpaper? "We only moved out here from Colorado a few months before . . ." She trailed off and let him fill in the rest.

"Ever think about moving back?"

She pasted a smile on her face. "Trying to get rid of me?" That sounded defensive. She added, "Moving's expensive. And I really don't have anyone out there, either. But I do miss it." Why had she said that? Maybe those blue eyes were making her babble. "I miss the snow," she heard herself confess.

"Stick around. Maybe you'll get some." She raised her eyebrows in surprise. "Usually about once or twice a winter, we'll have a little snowfall. But not enough to stick on the ground past lunchtime." He grinned that contagious grin, and she smiled back, relieved to get back to small talk. "If you drive through a neighborhood where kids live, you'll see the most pathetic snowmen on the lawns. Lumpy, about three feet tall, with dead grass poking out everywhere."

Meg laughed. "If we get snow, I'll be out there making one, too."

Their shared smile held, then dissolved into silence. "So," Craig said. "Any names picked out for the baby?"

"Jimmy. After my father."

"It's a boy? You know for sure?"

Meg nodded. "They did the sonogram two months ago."

Craig shook his head. "You're going to have your hands full."

"What do you mean?" She sounded defensive again, but she couldn't help it. "You think I can't handle a boy?"

"Don't get me wrong," Craig said. "Boys are just different. You've never been one."

"Social conditioning."

"Maybe. But which one of us is holding the screwdriver, and which one's baking the cake?" His grin eased the tension. "Trust me, you wouldn't want to try any cake I baked."

Meg let a smile come. She couldn't help it. She liked him. Liked him too much. "Don't speak too soon," she said. "You don't know if my cake is any better."

"Sure I do. It doesn't smell anything like burning charcoal." Standing, Craig pulled the diaper table into an upright position and jiggled it firmly to test the frame. It held solid. "Where does it go, here?" He inclined his head toward the bare section of wall she'd left for the table. She nodded, and Craig scooted it into place. It reached about two feet below the wallpaper border, just low enough to keep chubby little fingers from peeling away at the paper while she changed the baby.

Craig stood for a moment, considering the border. "I'll tell you something else you're better at than me." He nodded at the wallpaper, then turned his head to include the room in general. "This. I can fix what's wrong with a place, but when it comes to making it look right . . ." His eyes went to hers—still unrelentingly blue, and still opaque. Meg had no idea what was coming next. "I could use your help on something."

She frowned. "What?"

"I'm working on a place in Big Bear. That's up in the mountains, about an hour and a half from here." She'd heard of the town. "The house got damaged in a big quake over ten years ago, and it's been sitting ever since, so I got it for a song. I've fixed most of the damage, but what it's got now is a really bad case of the seventies—ugly shag carpet, green linoleum, that kind of thing." He fingered the slim white rail of the diaper table. "Want to drive up with me and take a look at it?"

She wasn't sure she followed him. "What for?"

"Your opinion. I want it to look nice, but I don't really know what to do with it." A smile stole over his face. "Plus, if you've been missing snow, they had a good storm up there a few days ago. I bet it's gorgeous right now."

Was he serious, or just offering a poor transplanted Colorado girl a trip up to see the snow?

"I could really use your opinion," he added. That smile prodded away at her resistance. "Just for a few ideas. I can't afford to pay a decorator."

He made it sound as if she'd be helping him, but Meg wondered. Who was doing whom a favor? And did she really want to drive an hour and a half in Craig's company?

She found that she did.

But she wasn't going to be a charity case. "I could make some fried chicken to take up for lunch," she offered.

"Sounds good to me." Craig gestured at his handiwork. "Well, Meg, what do you think? Have I earned my keep?"

Meg drew a deep breath as she felt an involuntary, stupid flutter in her chest. It had been months since she'd last heard a male voice call her Meg.

But this wasn't the junior prom. It was time to hold up her end of the bargain. "It's great. Thank you." Meg forced a normal tone into her voice. "That means I have a cake to frost." Putting her hands on the floor, she tried to push herself up from her sitting position, but failed on the first attempt. She'd forgotten, once again, about her extra bulk. These days she was always getting herself down into positions she had a hard time getting up from.

"Here." Craig reached down to offer a hand, and

smoothly pulled up all hundred-and-fifty pounds of her. The texture of his fingers was rough and firm; his hand was gentle and strong at the same time. Meg accepted the lift, then quickly let go.

It's just a trade, she reminded herself. *Like a business arrangement.* And she was about to pay up. She could operate on that basis and still be self-sufficient.

But there was no denying that, in that moment, it felt good to be helped up.

"You chased a cat across a lawn? In a car?" Meg's eyes sparkled.

It was fun making her laugh. "An ugly old Chevy," Craig said. "We called it the Wondermobile." He scraped some more chocolate frosting from his plate. Just as he'd suspected, the cake was lethally good.

"At least tell me it was a corner house."

He shook his head slowly. "Two doors down from the corner. Helen's lawn, as a matter of fact." He took another drink from his glass of milk. "I mowed her front yard for the rest of the summer, once my mom heard about it."

Meg started to pick up his plate, then stopped. "Do you want another piece? Or I can get it packed up to take with you."

Craig's mind warred. He shouldn't want another piece of cake. And he shouldn't want to stay. Shouldn't have stayed for this slice. The longer he stayed, the harder it was to remember which things she'd told him, and which ones he knew from the confessional. He was bound to trip up and give himself away sooner or later. Resolutely, he drained the last of his milk. "No, this was great. Thanks."

He followed her to the sink with his glass. As he watched her cross the kitchen floor, he couldn't resist a comment. "You're supporting another female stereotype, you know."

"What do you mean?"

He gestured downward. "Barefoot, pregnant and in the kitchen."

Meg looked at her feet. Apparently she'd forgotten she'd slipped out of her shoes back in the nursery.

She raised her chin, that playful gleam in her eyes. "It doesn't count," she told him haughtily. "I'm wearing socks."

Yes, he should have left some time ago. Things were starting to get too comfortable between them; they were having moments of real camaraderie. That wasn't what he'd planned on. Surely, at this point, he'd made up for eavesdropping when he'd never meant to, on information she didn't even know he knew. If he still wanted to ease his conscience, he should send a contribution to the Joshua Center and be done with it. Meg would appreciate that more, anyway; she seemed so quick to deflect any offer of help with some counteroffer to return the favor. Even when he'd asked for her advice on the Big Bear house, she'd had to up the ante by paying him off with lunch. Just for a simple drive up the mountains.

And why had he invited her up to Big Bear, anyway? She did seem to have a good eye for decorating, but he hadn't planned to get involved any further. *Involved*—there had to be another word for it. Involved with a pregnant woman? The idea was too outlandish to think about.

Meg rinsed their glasses and plates and put them into the dishwasher. "What was it with you, back then?"

It took him a second to regroup, to remember what they'd just been talking about. That's right, his old war stories. The ones that were fun to tell. "I think it's called 'adolescence.' "

"So what am I in for?" She turned around, her face serious now, as if bracing herself for the worst.

It was hard to imagine looking that far into the future, to a point when something as abstract as the baby in Meg's stomach would be a person big enough to drive a car. It was also hard to believe Meg would ask him for parenting advice. But he supposed he was the voice of experience, coming at it from the other side.

He raked a hand through the hair on the back of his head. "I don't know, Meg. Every kid is different." Her eyes stayed fixed on him, demanding more than evasion. "Just because I've been there, that doesn't make me an expert. It's not like I even plan on having kids."

"So you said."

So he had, that day when he'd dropped off the rocking chair. Well, now was a good time to get it understood again. While they were standing in the kitchen face to face.

"But I've never been a boy, remember?" Meg persisted. "So tell me about it."

Craig closed his eyes and tried to think. Was he really going to try to explain testosterone urges to a pregnant woman he barely knew? He hadn't been able to put it all into words when he was seventeen, either. Hadn't thought about it consciously at all. It had all come out as—action. He opened his eyes and drummed his fingers on the countertop. Action, again. He cleared his throat.

"I can only speak for myself, okay?" She nodded for him to go on. "Well, about the time I turned fifteen a lot of things happened. My mom got remarried, number one. I had the hots for just about any girl I looked at, number two. And when you can't do anything about it—" he couldn't believe he was saying all this "—there's a lot of pent-up energy."

He forced a smile, hoping Meg could fill in the blanks for herself. He didn't want to elaborate on the teen male libido. "About that time, you get a car. And you've got all these friends that are in the same kind of whacked-out shape you're in. So you do all kinds of crazy stuff. Goofy stuff, mostly. But—"

He turned around, facing the sink. The kitchen drain was rusty; it could stand to be replaced. "I guess I was mad. That's what the high school counselor said." Great. Now he sounded like a head case. "I mean, not mad as in crazy. Mad as in angry. I got into some trouble." He couldn't seem to stop his mouth. "Nothing really big, you haven't got a fugitive in your apartment . . . Anyway, I got caught lifting CDs at that little music store on First Street. If it'd been one of the big chains, it might have turned out a lot different. But this store called my mom, and they didn't press charges. That was over ten years ago. You know, I've never gone back in there again."

"Why were you mad?" Meg's voice, behind him, had gotten softer.

She was getting her revenge for that confession, big time. And she didn't even know it.

He turned back around, and nearly bumped into her pregnant stomach. She'd gotten closer, as if to—what? Give him a hug or something? Oh, no. Suddenly the tiny kitchen, with its enticing scent of chocolate and Meg's inviting warmth, felt very, very confining.

"Why was I mad?" he said flatly. "Because I spent thirteen years without a father. She left him when I was two, and I still don't know why. And when she got re-married, it was to this insurance salesman. A guy who couldn't throw a ball any better than she could. At least not as far as I knew. I never gave him a chance. I liked to work with my hands, he worked out of a briefcase—it was like we were from different planets."

They were face to face, and he had nowhere to go. All he could seem to do was keep talking.

"I guess I had some kind of fantasy about what my real father would have been like." He cast his eyes over Meg's shoulder, past the kitchen, into the faceless living room behind her. "You ought to put some pictures up. A kid should know his dad."

Meg didn't move, but something gleamed in her eyes, and this time it wasn't humor. He'd hurt her. What was wrong with him? He had a pretty good idea why she hadn't hung any pictures of Ron. "Look, all I can tell you is how it was for me," he said. "I'm not saying that's the way it's going to go for you. I just think a boy does better with a father."

Meg tried to digest the earful she'd just heard. It was daunting . . . but maybe now she'd be that much more prepared for what lay ahead.

Craig leaned his weight against the kitchen sink—as far away from her as he could get, she realized. "Anyway, I got over all that a long time ago. My mom's a great person. We get along fine. I've never been able to make friends with my step dad, but that's not his fault. It's just that with all that bad history, it's hard to start fresh." His expression lightened, as if the demons from his past had been scourged for the moment. Leaving her with a lot to think about. "I'm sorry. I wasn't trying to depress you."

"It's okay. I asked." Meg sneaked a finger to the corner of her eye. "What helped you the most? I mean—"

"What really bailed me out was the high school counselor. Not all the talking, I'm still not sure how much good that did. But he knew I liked to build things, or fix things. So he got me some work with the city, helping out on construction projects. Basic grunt work, at least at first. But it kept me out of trouble, got my hands busy." He shrugged. " 'The devil makes work for idle hands'."

Recognizing her line from the day he came to the Joshua Center, Meg managed a smile.

"The other part of it's just time," he said. "You grow up. Nobody's a teenager forever. Which means, the good news is, he'll settle down by the time he's, oh, twenty-two or so."

She gulped out a laugh.

"It's like I said. Every kid is different." His smile was crooked. "But it makes me a lousy candidate for a father. Just so you know."

Meg frowned. It was the second time he'd said that. Wait a minute. Was he suggesting—Did he think she was—

That was just embarrassing. Not to mention a little egotistical on his part.

She folded her arms. "Don't worry," she said, locking her eyes with his. "I'm not looking for one."

"Good." He crossed his arms in front of him, mirroring her stance. His lopsided grin stayed in place. "Glad we got that out of the way. So are we on for Big Bear, or what?"

Chapter Five

Downtown Victory looked different to Meg from the cab of Craig's pickup truck.

Partly, it was the vantage point, seeing everything from higher up. Partly, it was Craig's narration. He could tell her which Mexican restaurant used to be a pizza place before it was an ice cream parlor. When she listened to Craig on their way out of town for Big Bear, the aging business district took on the appearance of something valiantly struggling against the erosion of time.

They drove by a long, barn-red building that looked more like a ranch house, and Meg did a double take when she read the sign. "That's a veterinarian's office?"

"It is now. The residential area used to reach farther into town. A few of the businesses are converted houses. But most of the time they just tear down the house and start again."

Meg looked back over her shoulder at the tidy building, complete with wooden shutters and porch rail. "It's really cute."

He bobbed his head forward slightly. "Thank you."

"One of your projects?" Of course. Helen had told her Craig did a lot of construction downtown. "Any others?"

Craig's voice took on the inflection of an amusement park tour guide. "Well, coming up on your right, you'll see Vince's Spaghetti. . . ."

And it was just what it should be: a neat white building with red-and-white striped awnings, and a trellis climbing the wall next to the double doors. She looked at him accusingly. "You don't need my help."

"That's where you're wrong. I just worked with what was already there. There's a photo in the waiting area of what the place looked like in nineteen sixty four. I just copied that." He spared the restaurant one more glance in the rear view mirror. "I like old things."

"Me too." Meg leaned forward, watching on the left. "There's a little church around here, a Catholic church. I've always been curious about it. It looks like it's been there a long time."

Craig knocked on the side of his window. "Over here. Around the corner of Washington." He didn't elaborate. It seemed she'd finally hit on a building he didn't know anything about. Meg wondered what he'd think if he knew about her own odd little piece of history at that church. She'd left a part of her life behind that day in the confessional, or at least, she hoped so.

Victory faded behind them, replaced by long

stretches of empty fields and a few intermittent gas stations. Then Craig made another turn and they started a gradual climb. The desert's dry grass and Joshua trees slowly gave way to greener vegetation, and finally, pine trees. Meg sat up a little straighter, the dull ache in her lower back reminding her how long she'd been sitting.

"Look more like home?" Craig said. It was the first time either of them had spoken in half an hour.

"A little. Only home wouldn't be so green this time of year. Lots of bare aspen trees."

The climb continued, with steeper roads and more switch backs. Just when Meg began to wonder if the promised snow had already receded to a higher altitude, she saw the first patch of white at the side of the road. Within a few minutes, snow covered the ground and the rooftops on both sides of the road. She tried not to gape like a tourist; it hadn't been *that* long since she'd seen snow. Last winter she'd still lived in Denver with Ron.

Craig turned onto a street of houses with unpainted wood exteriors, giving them the feel of rustic mountain cabins. After a few minutes he pulled off the paved road, parking in the snow alongside the street in front of one of the houses. Like most of the others, it had a deliberately rough-hewn appearance, its wide panels of wood rounded slightly to look like logs.

And when Meg opened the door of the truck, she could have sworn she'd left Southern California behind. Cold, crisp air and the scent of pines greeted her, bringing back a lifetime of memories and associations.

She breathed in deeply as she took the big step down from the cab of the pickup.

Craig rounded the truck and halted when he reached her; from the way he stopped, Meg wondered if he'd meant to help her down. But he made no comment, just closed the door behind her and led her up the crunchy white front yard to the house.

As Craig unlocked the door, Meg wondered, not for the first time, what she was doing here. She would have liked to go to design school, but Craig didn't know that, and her plans had been cut short when her parents died. Now, presumably, she was supposed to walk into a house she'd never seen before and give him advice on what to do with it. What even qualified her to have an opinion?

Still, when she stepped inside as Craig held the door for her, one opinion formed very quickly.

"Ugh," she said, stepping onto the rust-colored shag carpet. Craig laughed behind her. Thank goodness he'd already told her he didn't like the carpet.

Even if it hadn't been a hideous shade of rust bordering on orange, the carpet would have needed replacing anyway. The first five feet from the front door were worn and matted from years of wet shoes tracking snow in.

Craig's laughter subsided. "I know, the orange shag was the first thing I wanted to get rid of. What color do you think you'd use?"

Before she opened her mouth again, Meg took in the rest of the room. A huge, beautiful stone fireplace covered most of one wall. Two other walls bore signs of recent plaster repairs. The living room was empty, but no matter what furniture went inside it, that fireplace would remain the room's unquestionable showpiece. "I don't think I'd use carpet at all," she said. "Not for the main entryway." She looked down at the beaten carpet under her feet. "Something that won't get soggy from the snow, and wouldn't be too slick for wet shoes. Maybe a rough granite, to tie in with the fireplace."

She bit her tongue. For someone who didn't know what she was talking about, she was talking an awful lot. She looked at Craig, but he was nodding, arms folded. "Come on. Let's move into the kitchen, if you want to be really appalled."

He took her by the elbow as he guided her into the next room. The unexpected touch surprised Meg; it seemed like such a courtly gesture. Maybe he expected her to fall over? If so, his support nearly backfired, setting Meg off balance as her heart raced.

Get a grip, girl. He's just walking you to the kitchen.

The room was as bad as Craig had promised. The cabinets were a cumbersome dark wood, and the curling linoleum had a dull olive green pattern. The appliances were dark brown, but that was better than the avocado green of the counter, which was made of some cheap veneer that was peeling up.

This time Meg tried to show some restraint. But as she glanced around the room, ideas started to take shape.

Craig seemed to know what she was thinking. "Go ahead. Play. Remember, this doesn't cost anybody anything, yet. I can always pick and choose, cut corners later."

Play. Meg took the invitation for what it was. She wasn't qualified to do anything else, anyway. So she transformed the kitchen in her mind's eye, and relayed the details to Craig: Clean white tile for the counter-tops. A light knotty pine for the cabinets. Old-fashioned brick for the floor.

Craig grinned. "And the appliances?"

Meg looked at the aging brown stove and sighed. "White," she admitted. "White never goes out of style." She surveyed the heavy earth-tone color scheme and tried to imagine how it had looked to the owners when it was first put in. "Hasn't this place been lived in at all since the seventies?"

"Well, it got used, but it was a rental cabin. A lot of the places up here are. After the quake damage, this one sat empty for almost ten years. No one needed it to live in, and I guess it wasn't easy to sell a cabin that needed so much work."

"Is that what you're going to use it for? A rental?"

"It's for my mother."

Meg closed her mouth before her jaw could hang open too long.

"It's not as outlandish as it sounds," Craig said. "I've always got a couple of jobs to keep the business going, plus I like to have one personal fixer-upper project on the side. Usually I fix something and sell it. But I've turned a profit on enough of those . . . and she deserves something nice. She can use it for a rental if she wants, or just a weekend getaway."

Meg frowned. "Not that I mind, but why don't you let her pick out what she wants for the place?"

"She doesn't know about it yet."

Meg picked her jaw up off the floor again. The man was fixing up a mountain retreat as a *surprise*? She was no expert, but it wasn't hard to guess he was still compensating for a misspent youth. "Are you sure you didn't burn down the house or something when you were growing up?"

Craig threw back his head and laughed. But that was the only answer she got.

Since there was no furniture, they ate cold chicken standing at the kitchen counter. Craig noticed Meg didn't attempt another sitting-on-the-floor position, nor did she take her shoes off in the kitchen. But she managed to take an awkward pose, like leaning one hip against the counter while she savored a drumstick, and make it look effortless.

She had nice ideas for the cabin, too. When Meg got wrapped up in her decorating schemes, a new light came into her eyes. With growing enthusiasm, she described her vision for each room until Craig could see it himself. He liked what he saw. Next, he'd have to see how affordable it was. If it worked out, maybe he'd bring her back up later on, when it was time to pick out things like curtains.

Just where was this going to end, anyway? For Craig, spending more time with Meg was like a killer returning to the scene of the crime. Did he subconsciously *want* to get caught? He doubted it. For one thing, he found himself forgetting his crime that day in the confessional. That made it all the more dangerous. The more he forgot to watch what he said, the more likely it was that he'd slip up. It was like waving a lit match near a fuse.

Still, there was no denying that an unorthodox friendship was developing between them. Meg grew less guarded all the time, and more fun to be with. Maybe it had been a long time since she'd had a real friend. Nothing wrong with that, he decided.

But that didn't explain why, near the end of the day, he felt his face go red when she suggested a wood-burning stove for the cabin's master bedroom. He could picture it, all right. The way this room would look by firelight, and the way firelight would look playing over long brunette hair, with Meg snuggled up in a big, warm bed, the covers rumpled all around her—

And this little ledge would be perfect for a coffee maker, she'd added, mercifully derailing that train of thought.

It was late afternoon by the time they were ready to go. Craig locked the door as Meg waited behind him. Before he could turn around, he felt a cold, wet, stinging smack on the back of his neck. He wheeled around with a yelp.

There Meg stood, halfway across the yard, beaming with obvious satisfaction over the snowball she'd just hurled. The natural thing to do was retaliate. Except, what kind of guy threw a snowball at a pregnant woman?

He narrowed his eyes at her. "Oh, not fair."

Meg stayed a safe distance away, still wearing that Mona Lisa smile, still clearly pleased with herself. She crossed her hands over her round stomach, practically defying him to strike back.

Inspiration struck. "You can't run, can you?" he said.

Meg took a step back. "You wouldn't."

"Oh, wouldn't I." Craig scooped up a double handful of snow and started purposefully toward her. He couldn't throw snow at her, couldn't chase her. But he was determined to make her as cold and soggy as he could.

Meg knew she was in trouble. Craig's longer legs ate up the short, snowy yard much faster than hers, and this time his ready grin had vengeance written all over it.

The truck. If she could get inside, maybe he'd think twice about getting snow all over the interior. She took the risk of turning her back, hurried the rest of the way across the yard and made it to the passenger door—

Locked.

She turned back around and found retribution looming over her: Craig stood two feet away, cupping the mass of snow in hands that had to be freezing. Meg shrank back against the truck, but there was no escape. She couldn't keep from giggling as their eyes locked.

For a moment, Craig didn't move, as though savoring his victory. Then the glint in his eyes seemed to soften. A tinge of mercy? Or something else? He stepped closer, and his eyes grew warmer. Meg sensed a new purpose behind his advance, something more dangerous than any snow attack. Something involving his lips and hers, and an embrace that could melt any snow. She should do something to stop it. But it wasn't just being physically cornered that held her stock still.

Craig let most of the snow fall to the ground between them—except for one handful. Slowly, his eyes never leaving hers, he formed a snowball and deposited it deliberately over her head, as though cracking an egg.

Meg shrieked as the snow cascaded over her hair, in front of her face, and down the back of her neck. He'd spared her a full dousing, but it was still plenty cold, thank you.

"Paybacks are murder," Craig intoned.

As the initial shock of the chill wore off, Meg knew what to do.

It was a dirty trick. She should have thought of it before. Clutching her stomach, she doubled over, bending her knees and dropping to crouch near the ground, where more snow waited. It got the expected reaction.

"Meg!" Craig bent over her. "Are you all right?"

His head was down close to hers. Perfect. As fast as she could, Meg scooped up a handful of snow and deposited it directly down the back of his neck.

Craig yowled and staggered off balance. Grabbing reflexively for something to hold on to, he took her down with him.

Before Craig knew what he was doing, he got a secure hold on Meg, clutching her against him as he fell backward onto the snowy front yard. He kept her on top of him, so that he bore the brunt of the fall and all of the snow.

Fear, annoyance, and relief all took turns pulling him into an uncomfortable knot. And still he held on to her, keeping her out of the snow. Protecting Meg and the baby, while his own jeans got soaked. It must be some crazy primal urge.

Meanwhile, on top of him, she was shaking with uncontrollable peals of near-hysterical laughter. Like someone who hadn't laughed in a long, long time.

He tried to fix her with a glare, but he doubted she could see it. She was still laughing too hard. "You scared me," he said.

"I'm sorry. I couldn't resist." Meg wiped at her eyes and pulled herself part way up. Then their eyes met, and for the first time, she seemed to realize just how closely their bodies were plastered together.

Her laughter died. For a moment her eyes held his, wide with some indescribable expression that held Craig spellbound, unable to move. Then her look gave way to something Craig could recognize, and appreciate: alarm. She tried again to pull herself up. Thanks to the slippery snow and her bulging middle, she fell back on top of him instead.

"Sorry," she gasped. "I'm like a beached whale."

Her giggles returned, and this time Craig welcomed

them. Anything to detract from the awkwardness of the moment. This had gotten *way* too close for comfort. He felt the hard swell of her stomach and the warmth of her body against his. Taking a deep breath, he grasped her shoulders and pushed her up. He hadn't bench-pressed any weights in a long time, but determination made up for lack of practice. Meg righted herself enough to stand up. Stray snow cascaded down her hair and her omnipresent red jacket, glittering like diamonds in the late afternoon sun.

"I'm sorry," she said again, but the latest wave of giggles hadn't stopped yet. He didn't know whether to be furious, or give in and laugh himself.

"Thanks for catching us," she added.

Us. She was exactly right. He'd taken the fall, quite literally, for both Meg and the baby. It had been complete, total, pure reflex. And Craig knew he didn't have a paternal bone in his body. It was just caveman instinct. That was more chilling than the snow still seeping into his jeans. He stood up and brushed himself off.

"If you don't mind," he said, not meeting her eyes, "I'll just put on a dry pair of pants." He retrieved his spare jeans from the back of the truck—a handy thing, he'd learned, in his line of work—and left her waiting outside while he went back into the house to change.

Chapter Six

The pale lights of the Victory Mall loomed ahead as they reached the last leg of the trip home. "Want to stop for a bite?" Craig asked. The invitation surprised Meg, and she hesitated before answering.

The drive back down to Victory had started out as a quiet one. Meg wasn't sure if Craig's silence was because of her faked emergency or his snow-soaked jeans, but she decided she wasn't up to finding out. What had gotten into her? Somehow she'd regressed into a child, and clearly he wasn't amused. But she'd already apologized. So she settled for enjoying the view of the vanishing snow while it lasted, and then of the mountains themselves in the waning sunlight.

By the time the snow thinned away, Craig's mood had thawed enough to offer her a choice of the CDs stashed in the large glove compartment of his truck. Fortunately, Craig's taste in music wasn't too far from hers. Lots of upbeat rock, no hard-core heavy metal or rap. She found a Bruce Springsteen hits collection, and that made her choice easy. Good music could fill any silence.

Now, sliding the truck into the right-hand lane of Desert Valley Boulevard, Craig nodded at the mall up ahead. "The food court has something for everybody," he persisted.

Meg glanced at him sideways and glimpsed the curve of his smile. This must be his way of offering an olive branch. And the mall's food court did have a good submarine sandwich shop, with whole wheat bread and plenty of fresh vegetables. Not a bad choice for the baby. "Okay."

"I discovered another difference between boys and girls, by the way," Craig said as they pulled into a parking space.

"Oh?"

He shut off the engine. "No girl should ever sing 'Born to Run.'"

She'd forgotten herself, Meg realized, and felt her cheeks warm. But it was nice to have Craig's good humor back.

Going through the doors of the mall, they passed from the chilly desert evening into an oasis of artificial trees. The mall decorators had done their best to turn the food court into a tropical paradise, as if to compensate for the sparse landscape outside. Meg gestured at the plastic forest. "You know you're back in Victory," she said, "when you see more trees inside than outside."

Craig chuckled as he surveyed the signs above them

in the small, hexagonal food court. "You know you're back in Victory," he said, "when you have eight fine fast food restaurants to choose from, and three of them sell hamburgers. What sounds good to you?"

"The Sub Stop."

Craig made a face. "Too healthy for me. Want to split up, and meet back here?"

Meg agreed, and they went to order their respective meals from different vendors. When she got her sandwich, Meg found Craig standing by a table he'd already claimed for them, near the raised dais where the food court's resident piano player sat.

She grinned and headed over. She would have picked the same spot herself. Before Meg moved here, she'd never seen a mall with a piano player, not even in her own beloved Midwest. She had no idea how much they paid him—a friendly-faced man who played skillful, jazzy improvisations of pop tunes—but it couldn't be anywhere near what he was worth.

"You know you're back in Victory," Craig said as she joined him, "when they've got a piano player at the mall."

Meg took her seat. "Score one for Victory."

Yes, the mood had lightened considerably. As they started to eat, the memory of their snow scuffle seemed to be behind them. Except when Meg met Craig's eyes by accident, and remembered the way they'd fixed on her in that moment when she'd realized their bodies were so close. She felt a rush of goose bumps at the memory, and that was absolutely insane. She'd even imagined he wanted to kiss her. In her condition, that had to be the furthest thing from Craig's mind. Meg had heard some women got more lustful when they were pregnant. That must be her problem.

Just what she needed.

Returning to the present, she looked toward the piano player again. "How long has he been playing here?"

"About three years. Before that they had an older lady who made everything sound like "On Top of Old Smokey.'"

Meg giggled. "And before that?"

He shook his head. "The mall's only been open six years, believe it or not."

"And you've lived here for how long?"

Craig squinted upward at the mall's skylight ceiling. "Twenty-one years. Since I was seven. I started first grade here."

She tried to picture Craig as a first-grader and got an image of a dark-haired little boy, his hair slicked back by a wet comb. "You don't remember your father at all?"

Craig brought his head back down to meet her eyes, his brows raised. "Where'd that come from?"

Oops. "I don't know. Just thinking." *About your mom sending you off to school all on her own. . . .* No, judging by his expression, he wouldn't want to hear that.

His face relaxed back into the familiar grin. "Sorry. It's just, you've heard enough of my life story already."

Craig nudged his package of French fries to the edge of his food tray, toward Meg. She started to reach for one, then snatched her fingers back. This was supposed to be her healthy meal for the day. If she didn't behave herself, Jimmy was going to be born with acne, and she'd weigh two hundred pounds even after the delivery.

Meg caught a glimpse of an approaching baby stroller, and the sight pulled her gaze like a magnet. She searched for the baby who had to be hidden under the piles of pink blankets. By the time she recognized the short woman with light brown hair who was pushing the stroller, it was too late.

Meg remembered something else about the Victory Mall. One reason she hadn't been here in a while.

You were bound to run into someone you knew.

And sweet though she was, Lori Kramer, the secretary from Ron's church, wasn't someone Meg wanted to see right now. Not in her present, pregnant, widowed state. For all these months, she'd managed to avoid running into anyone connected with Ron. But Meg had been so busy trying for a glance at the baby, she'd given Lori ample time to recognize her.

"Megan!" Lori wheeled across the remaining tile squares between them, rounded the table past Craig, and bent to scoop her into a fierce, one-arm hug.

Meg returned the hug, but stayed planted in her chair. If she didn't get up, maybe Lori wouldn't notice her extra midsection.

Maybe ostriches could drive sports cars.

"Meg," Lori's voice came from behind her shoulder. "I haven't seen you in so long! How are you—" She straightened to get a better look at Meg, and her voice died in her throat. Of course the pregnancy hadn't gone unnoticed.

As if Meg had really stood a chance of keeping the news about the baby from reaching the church for a whole nine months. She couldn't even keep it hidden under a table at the mall for more than twenty seconds. But if there was one thing Meg didn't want, it was a fresh tide of well-wishers who knew and admired Ron, standing by to offer condolences and help to his grieving, expectant widow.

She felt like a phony already.

Lori blinked, visibly trying to recoup. "Meg," she said again. "I didn't know—"

Another hug, this time with both arms, as Lori let go of the baby stroller. Sympathy, congratulations, or a mere loss for words? Whatever it was, it sparked an unexpected reaction. Meg felt tears prickle behind her eyelids.

"Honey," Lori pulled back again, blinked again. "You didn't tell anybody! How are you feeling? You look great!" She returned a hand to the baby stroller, rolling it closer. The stroller gave Meg the diversion she needed.

"I'm fine," she said. "How's the baby?"

Automatically, Lori's eyes went down to the mound of blankets in the stroller. She pulled back a crocheted edge to reveal a sweetly sleeping face with delicate brown eyelashes. Meg did her math. Lori's baby shower had only been a few weeks before Ron's death, and Lori had been . . . about as pregnant as Meg was now. Unexpected tears stung again. She ignored them and finished her calculations. "She's about eight months now, right?"

Lori nodded.

"She's beautiful," Meg said wholeheartedly. The soft-looking cheeks just begged to be touched, but she didn't dare risk disturbing such a peaceful slumber. "You were naming her 'Tabitha,' right?" The last time Meg went to church, the baby still hadn't been born.

"Little Tabby," Lori agreed. She smoothed down the edge of the blanket, but left the baby's face exposed for further viewing. Meg studied her, mesmerized. Soon enough, Jimmy would be born, but sometimes all the months of waiting seemed like forever. Lori said, "Now, what about you?"

Meg had dropped her guard. Her reprieve was over. And Lori was sinking into a third, unoccupied chair at their table. "Oh, sweetie, you have to let me put together a shower for you. How soon—"

"It's okay." Meg remembered that she had an audience of two—not counting the sleeping baby in the frill-covered stroller—and that Craig hadn't said a word since Lori arrived. She sneaked a quick glance his way; he was sitting back in a quiet, wait-and-see posture. Not much help there. Meg protested, "You don't have to do that."

"Who said anything about having to? I *want* to." Lori's eyes wavered between enthusiasm and hurt. Meg bit her lip.

Why was Craig silently devouring the scene in front of him?

And what else did she expect him to do?

She had one dirty rotten trump card to play. Reluctantly, she used it. Meg lowered her eyes. "It's just—it would remind me too much of Ron."

"Oh, honey." Oh, no. More sympathy. Every time Meg opened her mouth, she made this worse. "You'll enjoy your baby. I know you will. Take lots of pictures. I've already filled two albums. If you want to learn about scrapbooking, I can show you how. And if you need anything—baby-sitting, or help at home after the baby's born—"

No, no, no. "I'm all right. Really."

"Meg?" After a long absence, Craig's voice came from across the table. She turned. "You haven't introduced us," he said.

It was a welcome change of subject, at least. But it brought up another problem, something Meg hadn't thought of before. Would Lori think that Craig . . . that she and Craig . . . ?

Surely not. Just because he was a male within a few feet of her, surely Lori wouldn't get any wild ideas about anyone besides Ron being the baby's father.

Lori turned toward Craig. "I'm so sorry." If any suspicion lurked behind those wide eyes, it didn't show. "I was the rude one. I was so excited to see Meg I barely saw you." She held out her hand. "I'm Lori Kramer. A friend of Meg's from church."

As Craig introduced himself to Lori, Meg realized she had another problem. The tall fruit smoothie she'd gotten with her sandwich was playing havoc with her pregnant bladder. Maybe the problem could be part of the solution.

"I'm sorry," she said, standing. "I need to use the rest room." She smiled at Lori. "You remember how it is, right?"

And she escaped, leaving Craig on his own to handle the conversation for the next few minutes. If Lori was still there when she returned, at least this gave her a few minutes to regroup. And she didn't think Craig could make any more of a hash of it than she already had.

But it was one more thing she'd owe him for.

He'd been seen with Meg in public before, but this was the first time Craig wished he had a T-shirt with the words *It's Not Mine* emblazoned across his chest.

He'd never been one for worrying about what people thought. Not once his mom remarried and he hit high school, anyway. But this wasn't about what people thought of Craig. It was about what people, this chatter-box from church in particular, might think of Meg.

Meg, who'd deserted him for who-knew-how-long for a trip to the ladies' room and, Craig guessed, a chance to come up for air. She was going to get payback for more than just a snowball fight by the time this was through.

At first he'd half expected Lori to tag along—didn't women always travel to rest rooms in packs?—but she stayed put, one hand resting protectively on the handle of the stroller. One of those awkward silences arose, the kind that tend to come up between people with absolutely nothing to say to each other. But, as Craig might have anticipated, it wasn't in Lori Kramer's nature to stay silent for very long.

"I haven't seen Meg in forever," Lori said. "She's such a nice person."

Craig nodded. "Very nice." He kept his tone neutral. He didn't know what she might be reading into his relationship with Meg, but it wouldn't take a rocket scientist to guess.

"She gave me the most thoughtful gift at my baby shower," Lori went on. "You know how at a shower, everyone gives you gifts for the baby, of course. Well, her present had a really cute rattle for a package topper. But inside was this beautiful silky nightie. For me. With buttons down the front, so it was something I could use right away, after the baby was born."

"Buttons down the—" The significance escaped him until he saw Lori's ears turn pink. Oh, right. Nursing. Craig cleared his throat.

Lori let out a little giggle. "Anyway. She's just like that. You saw how she remembered the baby's name. And she's never even *seen* Tabby before."

Craig nodded again; little else seemed to be required to keep up a conversation with Lori. Anyway, no one needed to sell him on Meg as a nice person. And then he realized that was just what Lori Kramer was doing—salesmanship. Matchmaking. Why, sure. Maybe she could fix up the lonely pregnant woman with the probably-single man across the table. If Lori Kramer was as transparent as she seemed, maybe she wasn't anything to worry about.

But then she shifted gears on him. The giggle went, and so did the salesmanship, replaced by a serious look. "How is she doing, really?"

"Good, as far as I know. We just met a couple weeks ago." There. That was a good piece of information to get in there.

"Oh?" Her avid eyes brightened. "How did you meet?"

He explained, briefly, how he'd let a pregnant woman share his table at a crowded restaurant, and Lori reacted as if he'd rescued her friend from a burning building. At that point, thankfully, Meg reappeared. If she was less than happy to see Lori still there, she didn't show it. She seated herself with a smile, composure apparently restored for the moment.

The moment wouldn't last for long, if Lori had anything to do with it. "I was just thinking," Lori said. When did she have time to think? During Craig's inspirational story about the Mojave Burger meeting? "Have you signed up for a Lamaze class yet?" Craig stiffened. Lamaze. Wasn't that another breast-feeding thing? "Do you have a labor coach?"

Oh. Lamaze, as in natural childbirth.

That was worse.

Meg's smile faltered. "I hadn't thought about it yet."

Lori's eyebrows raised in faint alarm. "You should. It's a six-week course. You ought to be in a class already. When are you due?"

"In about five weeks." Meg put her smile back on, but it didn't hold as firm this time. "I guess I figured I'd read some books. I've kind of been skipping those chapters up to now."

Hadn't thought about it yet? With the nursery decorated and ready to go? That didn't sound like Meg.

"I read books, too," Lori said. "But you really need the class. It helped me a lot."

"You think it's that important?" Meg said.

Lori nodded solemnly, and Craig thought he saw Meg's color fade a notch. Hadn't her doctor talked to her about any of this? "Not to scare you or anything," Lori said. "But knowing those exercises, having something to focus on—it made a big difference. Do it. But you'd better call quick, while they can still fit you into a class."

Meg's face, like Lori's, had taken on a solemn set. Craig toyed briefly with the idea of nudging the stroller with his foot, setting the baby off, and derailing this conversation. But he couldn't quite bring himself to do it.

Lori seemed to sense the thoughts behind Meg's expression. "Do you need a coach?"

Meg was silent. Craig had a brief, selfish moment of panic, when he was sure Lori was about to turn around and volunteer him for the job.

Instead, Lori said, "If you need somebody, I can do it."

Meg shook her head. "I couldn't—"

Lori rested a hand on Meg's. "Really. I'd be glad to." The perky smile returned. "After all, you won't let me give you a baby shower."

To Craig's surprise, Meg said, "I'll think about it."

"Just let me know. But make sure you call the hospital first thing." Lori watched Meg's silent face, and once again surprised Craig by reading her correctly. "You don't always have to be strong, sweetie. This is one time where it's good to have someone there to help. Think about it. You can call me at the church office." She stood and gave Meg one more hug before she departed with her stroller.

Craig stared after Lori with a little more respect. For someone who didn't appear to be very close to Meg, she'd shown pretty good insight into Miss Stop-Being-Nice-to-Me, I'll-Pay-You-Back-with-Chocolate-Cake-and-Chicken.

As Lori and her stroller faded toward the mall's exit doors, Craig asked, "How well do you two know each other?"

"Not that well." Meg shook off a new sense of apprehension. She *had* been putting off dealing with the details of the delivery. Her doctor had given her a handout about Lamaze classes; unlike everything else to do with the pregnancy, she'd buried it somewhere in a stack of papers. Denial. She knew and accepted that she'd be raising a baby alone, but she didn't want to think about going through the birth process alone. She leaned her elbow on the table and rested her head against her hand.

The other half of her vegetarian sub sat in front of her. It didn't look as appetizing as it had half an hour ago.

Craig nudged his bag of French fries in her direction again. Meg peered up into the blue eyes that, as usual, seemed to see way too much. The empathetic look was hard to resist. But at least she could turn down the junk food. She smiled weakly. "No, thanks."

Craig plucked a fry from the stack. She wondered if they were still warm. "So, are you going to take her up on the labor thing?"

"Maybe." Meg sipped her smoothie. "I probably should."

"Really? You think you can handle Miss Mary Sunshine for a coach?"

"She's not so bad. I know she can come across a little . . ."

"Giggly? Nosey?"

Meg protested, "She's really a nice person."

"She said the same thing about you. Maybe you should form a mutual admiration society," Craig said. "So why is it you looked ready to dive under the table when she came running up here? Or didn't I bail you out when you went running to the rest room?"

Meg studied her sandwich's paper wrapping. "It's—complicated."

"So what *is* the deal?" he said. His voice had a more gentle tone now; something about it had her eyelids prickling again, for the third time tonight. Her hormones must be going crazy. Craig persisted. "What sends you running away from perfectly nice, harmless church ladies?"

She blinked hard and tried to fix him with a meaningful glare. "I had to go to the bathroom."

"That's complicated?"

Meg's glare faltered. She picked up a French fry. Just one.

"Come on, Meg. What is it that's got you staying away from church and ducking people all these months?"

She frowned. "How would you know?"

Craig took a long drink from his coke. Then he shrugged. "It's obvious."

"How do you know I haven't been going to church?"

"Well, you were with me last Sunday, for one thing. Getting your diaper table built." He rattled the ice in his drink. "And Lori said you'd never seen the baby before. Somehow I don't think you could go that long without noticing a baby."

"Pretty observant of you."

"I'm an observant kind of a guy." Craig rattled his cup once more, and decided there was nothing worthwhile left inside, and set it down. "I'm a pretty good listener, too, if you want to talk." He leaned back in his chair, as if he had all the time in the world.

Where had this inquisitive Craig come from? And what was he trying to do to her? His eyes held hers, unflinching. Rock steady. There was something so solid about Craig, always tempting her to lean on him. Just a little. And not just for drives up to the mountains, or baby furniture construction. Those were tangible things. The kind of support Craig represented was much more insidious. And much more dangerous. Leaning on Craig would feel so good. The trouble with leaning was that when someone stopped being there, you fell over.

Meg remained silent, like a criminal exercising her Miranda rights.

To her relief, after several beats, Craig's eyes lost their intensity and crinkled into a smile. "So, do you want any more fries?"

Meg's hand wavered in mid-air above the pile of French fries. There were only a few left. Apparently she'd just devoured most of them without even knowing it.

Craig's teasing grin was almost worse than his scrutiny had been. Did he have to look so satisfied?

She raised her chin at him. "You could have at least ordered fried zucchini. Then I could pretend there were some vitamins in there somewhere." Meg sat back, putting the fries out of her reach.

"You're nervous about it, aren't you? The labor, I mean."

"A little. I guess that's why I haven't thought about it." Meg shrugged. "I'm sure it'll be a tough day. But afterward, there's this reward that lasts forever." She had to remember that. Keep Jimmy in mind. Instead of throwing snowballs at some handsome stranger who wasn't going to be part of their lives.

"Lori was right about one thing, you know," Craig said. "Nobody expects you to be the Rock of Gibraltar."

Meg resumed her cautious silence.

Craig cocked an eyebrow. "Or, we could do it your way. Stop by the Air Force base, and see if they'll lend you a bullet to bite on. Then we could scout out a field for you to birth the baby in—"

That was better. She felt a smile sneak across her face.

"—and if you want to go for the luxury plan, we could send someone out there after you to boil water and tear sheets."

Meg laughed. Things were back to normal.

Craig saw Meg safely to the door of her apartment, then got himself safely back into the cab of his pickup. He couldn't, for the life of him, imagine why he kept trying to walk into Meg's problems with both feet.

When he started the engine, the CD player came back on. Craig turned up the music and filled the truck with it.

The big blue pickup wasn't your standard-issue cruising vehicle. But climbing back on the freeway ramp with the blare of rock behind him brought back memories, some of them good. Tonight it felt right to be out on the road with almost no traffic ahead of him, as if he could put distance between himself and—something.

Why had he grilled Meg like that? As if she was going to spill her guts about a loveless marriage to someone she barely knew. As if he'd want her to.

The chorus kicked in, and he turned up the stereo.

He was tired of watching what he said, trying not to let on that he knew more than he was supposed to know, more than he had any right to know. It was none of his business and it wasn't his problem.

He'd heard labor hurt. Really, really hurt.

Craig shoved those thoughts aside, and let the music and the night and the lights of the road wash over him.

Until he saw another light, this one in his rearview mirror: a pulsing blue light. That brought back memories, too.

He swore under his breath and eased up on the accelerator—for all the good it would do him now—and obediently pulled over. It had been years since he'd been stopped like this; he tried to remember what else to do. At least he didn't have to check to see if one of his buddies had cracked a beer open in the back seat against his orders.

When he looked over his shoulder to see who was walking up to the driver's side door, the sense of deja vu was complete. It was Officer Rivera. He wasn't sure if that was good or bad.

"Craig." The California Highway Patrol officer peered in the window at him. "You and I haven't done this in a long time." In the dim light from the CHP cruiser, the officer's white teeth glinted with a bit of humor.

Craig squirmed and tried to smile back.

What he'd said was true enough. Last time he'd seen Officer Rivera, Craig had been working on renovations in the courthouse lobby a few months ago. They'd seen each other on an almost daily basis then, a smile and a nod, and once or twice Craig had found himself thinking how times had changed.

Now he was back where he'd started, feeling like a stupid punk kid. It could have been ten years ago. No, twelve. Except that even in the flickering light from the top of the squad car, he could see some gray streaks at Officer Rivera's temples that hadn't been there before. Funny he hadn't noticed that at the courthouse. Of course, at the courthouse, he hadn't had such a hard time meeting the cop's eyes.

"You were doing close to eighty."

"Sorry." Craig smiled sheepishly. "I guess I just lost track of how fast I was going." And it was the truth. Just an honest, everyday citizen, going a little too fast. It didn't ease the old familiar knot in his stomach.

"Got your license and registration?"

Craig handed them over, and the officer put them on a clipboard. "Be right back."

Craig endured the familiar, interminable wait while the officer went to his car and radioed back to headquarters. Checking him for warrants? They wouldn't find anything. He had to remember that. There was nothing to worry about this time. No call to his mother, no threat of a license suspension, no big deal. This could be one expensive ticket, and it might make his insurance rates go haywire, but it was a one-time thing. Not a recurring habit, not any more.

After several minutes, Rivera returned and handed back Craig's license and registration. "Here you go," he said, tearing a slip of paper from the clipboard. "It's just a warning. You be more careful."

Craig met Officer Rivera's eyes, what he could see of them in the dim light, and caught that glint of a smile again.

Speechless, Craig took the narrow yellow slip and watched the officer start back to his cruiser. Slowly, Craig realized what had happened. Rivera hadn't talked to him like a punk kid. He'd talked to him like a grown man.

"Raul," Craig ventured. He knew the man's first name. He'd read it on his badge enough times.

Rivera turned with a look of slight surprise.

"Thanks," Craig said. Man to man.

Rivera nodded once, just once, and strolled back to the cruiser.

Craig started the truck, turned the stereo back up, and continued the drive home, keeping his eye on the speedometer all the way.

Chapter Seven

"Wednesday night?" Lori's voice faltered on the other end of the telephone line, and Meg knew that wasn't a good sign.

She tightened her grip around the phone in the back room of the Joshua Center, a stack of filing forgotten in front of her. She'd called Lori to tell her she'd enrolled in the last Lamaze class the hospital had to offer before Jimmy was due. Even though Meg had missed the first three weeks, the class instructor had agreed to squeeze her in, apparently feeling that half a Lamaze class was better than none. She'd promised to load Meg down with literature and workbooks to cover what she'd missed. Oh, joy.

Now it sounded like her volunteer coach couldn't make it.

Lori sounded as dismayed as Meg felt. "My boss has me going to a seminar for work Wednesday nights. It's mandatory. Darn it, Meg, I never thought—"

"It's okay," Meg said quickly. "I can get—" Who? Meg hadn't let herself get close to many people since Ron's death. She remembered all those sympathetic hugs, those first few Sundays at church after the funeral, and shuddered. One thing about Lori: she didn't seem to think of Meg exclusively as The Widow Reilly.

Meg tried to keep the desperation out of her voice. "I'll find somebody."

"Ron doesn't have any family in town, right?"

"No." Ron's parents had both passed away before he and Meg even met.

"Let me think." Distant fingernails tapped on some surface. "All you need is someone to be there in class with you, to help you count the breaths and stuff. But I can be there with you for the delivery. I just had Tabby. I remember all that stuff."

Meg hesitated.

"I mean it," Lori said. "I wouldn't miss it. Come heck or high water, I'll get there when that baby's born. I promise. Even if you decide to give birth on a Wednesday night, I can miss one class." Her omnipresent giggle returned. "How does that sound?"

Heck or high water, Meg mused. Coming from Lori, that probably amounted to a blood oath.

"It's a deal," Meg said.

"Great. Here's my cell phone number. I want you to have it right now, just in case." Lori recited the number. "And think about the scrapbooking, okay? I'm having a class at my house next Monday night. It's really fun.

Just bring five or ten pictures from some event—a birthday, vacation, or whatever—and I can get you started. And I'll feed you lots of snacks. See if you can make it."

Meg nodded numbly before she remembered she was on the phone. "Okay. Thanks, Lori. For everything."

After they hung up, she stared at the papers she'd been alphabetizing. For a moment the names on the forms, even the alphabet itself, lost all meaning.

It would be all right, Meg told herself. She had a labor coach to see her through the actual delivery. Someone who'd already been through it, and knew what to expect.

All she needed now was a classmate.

Craig climbed out of his truck with Meg's cake pan and walked into the front office of the Joshua Center.

Helen was on the phone, but she quickly put her call on hold to go into the back room and retrieve Meg. Was it his imagination, or did every female on the planet suddenly seem anxious to throw him together with Meg?

He shouldn't have picked lunchtime to return Meg's cake pan, but for some reason, he had. Maybe it was Pavlovian. Thursday afternoons meant Mojave Burger and Meg. What could it hurt? It wasn't like he was going to get romantically involved with a pregnant woman, no matter what the Helens and Loris of the world had in mind.

Besides, maybe she'd already eaten.

Meg emerged and looked at the cake pan as if she didn't recognize it. Then her eyes seemed to focus, and she smiled. "For me? You shouldn't have."

He knew that expression. It was the same fixed smile she'd given to Lori the other day at the mall.

"Thanks again for the cake," he said lamely. "It was great."

Helen was back on the phone. "I tried to tell her that. I said, 'Why are you buying beige carpet?'"

Meg took the cake pan. "You don't mean it took you this long to finish the cake."

"Not near," he admitted. "It just took me that long to wash it." Meg chuckled, but she still seemed distracted. Craig said, "Have you had lunch yet?"

Meg looked at Helen uncertainly, as if she couldn't remember whether or not she'd eaten. Helen shouldered the mouthpiece with one hand, and waved her away with the other. "I'm fine here. Just let me know if you need me for that class." Back into the phone, she said, "Beige carpet. You *know* the kids are going to throw up red Kool-Aid on it. You'd think she'd remember. When she was four, she vomited Cocoa Puffs all over the—"

Craig nodded toward the door. "On that note . . ."

Meg retrieved her purse from the back room, then scooted to join him without speaking. She didn't seem upset with Craig, but clearly, something was on her mind. Something about that class Helen mentioned?

Outside, Craig boosted her up into his truck. She let

him help her up, but never down. Every time he got out of the truck, she was already out the door by the time he made it to her side.

Craig climbed in beside her and nodded back toward the Joshua Center. "What was that about?"

"What?"

"With Helen." Craig pulled out of the parking space.

"Well, I guess when her daughter was little she threw up Cocoa Puffs on—"

"Not that. What was she saying about a class?"

"Oh, that." Meg looked out the window. "She said she'd do the Lamaze class with me."

Helen? The woman meant well, Craig knew that. He'd grown up down the street from her, and she'd been there for his mother more times than he could count. But she could also put a negative spin on anything. "Are you kidding? Stick with Miss Mary Sunshine."

"That's the problem. I can't."

By the time Meg had finished explaining about conflicting classes and Lamaze coaches, they'd pulled into the parking lot at Mojave Burger. Craig shut off the engine, beset by the feeling of being backed into a corner. She hadn't come right out and asked, but it was obvious she needed someone.

He wasn't going to do it. No way. He'd be out of his mind.

But somewhere along the line, this had turned into more than guilt about something he'd heard accidentally in a confessional. He liked Meg, and as calmly as she talked about it, he could tell she was scared. Worried. Nervous about what was ahead of her.

Meg turned to open her door—without his help, as usual—and he put his hand on her arm. She jumped at the contact, and Craig felt a little electric power surge, too. He ignored it.

"Wait," he said.

If she took the class with Helen she'd have three weeks of horror stories to listen to. Craig could help her keep it light, distract her from the gory details. And what was three weeks worth of Wednesday nights, anyway?

"I'll do it," he said.

She looked at him blankly. "Do what?"

She hadn't asked him, clearly hadn't even been thinking about asking him. Craig lifted his arm away. "I'll get the door for you," he said. "It's pretty far up, and I always think about you tripping and—" He nodded toward her stomach.

There. He was off the hook. A miss was as good as a mile.

"Oh." Meg smiled and stayed put. So did Craig, struck by the instant switch in her attitude. She'd accept his help with the door now, because he'd given her a reason even she couldn't disagree with. It wasn't for her. It was for the baby.

But she didn't have any trouble accepting help from Lori and Helen. What was up with that? He'd be more help to her than Helen. Helen would make her a nervous wreck. Heck, under less trying circumstances, Helen would make *him* a nervous wreck.

His tongue blundered ahead of him. "I meant something else, too. The class." Her blank look returned. "If you want another partner for that childbirth class—"

"You?" Meg's voice was incredulous.

This was getting downright insulting. "Listen. If you take the class with Helen, she's going to make you nuts. She'll give you an earful of everything that could possibly go wrong. You don't need that." In search of something solid for support, his left hand gripped the steering wheel. "You did say Lori was going to coach you for the actual delivery, right?"

"Right."

"So?" Craig put his other hand on the wheel. When he heard himself say it, it made perfect sense to him.

He watched as Meg's eyes got wider and started darting around the cab of the truck. "Craig, I can't ask you to do that. There's no way I could pay you back for—"

"What is it with you and paying people back?" His hands tightened around the wheel. "How were you going to pay Lori back? Make her a batch of muffins? Redecorate her living room?"

Meg stared at Craig in disbelief. He seemed almost angry. And he'd asked her a question she couldn't answer. Why pay Craig back, and not Lori or Helen? Because Lori was the church secretary, doing her part to serve God? Because Helen was roughly her mother's age, and the first person she'd talked to after she hung up the phone with Lori? Or was it because Craig was a man?

Not just any man. Someone who made her laugh. Who made her hot and bothered, at a time in her life when she shouldn't be. Someone who tempted her to need someone again. She couldn't go that route.

"It's a woman thing," she said.

"Fine." Craig opened his door.

He seemed annoyed, but she couldn't imagine why. Surely he wasn't anxious to sit in on a class full of pregnant women. Apparently, somehow, she'd offended him with her system of tit for tat. But it couldn't be helped.

Meg opened her door, ready to climb out, then remembered and waited.

Craig came around and reached up a hand. She said, "Look, I didn't mean to offend you."

Craig held her by the elbow, and she took the big step down from the truck. *For the baby,* she reminded herself, ignoring the heat that raced up her arm.

"No offense taken." Craig's tone was casual, but something in his eyes was just a fraction cooler than usual. "It's up to you. It's your baby." He shrugged and herded her toward the restaurant. His eyes might be cool, but his touch was still warm on her arm. And Meg had to admit it felt good there.

The more she saw Craig, the more she weakened. She should have stuck to her brown-bag lunch back at the Joshua Center, even though visions of grilled chicken sandwiches had begun haunting her even before she called Lori.

Craig finally let go of her arm to open the door of the restaurant.

At the table, he nudged his bag of French fries toward the middle again. Meg stared at them. This time, she wouldn't. She shouldn't. Lunch at Mojave Burger, grilled chicken or not, was bad enough. She was eating too much fast food these days.

"Ketchup?" Craig said, interrupting her stare-out with the fries.

"Oh. No, thanks." A silence stretched out. What would they be talking about if he hadn't brought up the Lamaze coaching thing?

"The thing is," she said, "I have to be able to take care of myself."

"Oh, are we back to that?" Craig shook his head. "Forget it."

But Meg couldn't forget it. For one thing, Craig had a point. Helen had a heart of gold, but Meg wasn't looking forward to three weeks of classes with the kind of commentary only Helen could provide. Only, who else was there?

People who'd known Ron, and now revered him. People who would have all kinds of questions about where she'd been hiding herself all this time. People who'd heap sympathy on her until it felt like coals of fire on her head—and who'd be horrified if they knew how things had really left off between her and Ron.

"What I don't get," Craig said, "is why this spiked fence goes up around you any time I try to help you. Like it's some kind of a trap."

Meg raised her eyes, taken aback by both his bluntness and his insight. "It is a trap," she said. "For me, anyway. Every time I start to count on someone, they die." She hadn't meant for it to come out like that. It sounded like The Curse of Meg.

Craig's head jerked up. "Everyone?"

Meg lowered her eyes. "Well, there was Ron. And before that, my parents."

Craig felt like he'd been slapped. What an idiot he was. Where had he thought her parents were while their daughter was pregnant and alone? Off skiing in Colorado? Sunning themselves on the Fiji Islands? He swallowed hard. "What happened?"

"A car accident. When I was eighteen."

"Oh, crap. I mean, I'm sorry. I never thought about it." He passed a hand roughly through his hair. He'd thought he had it tough, having only one parent.

"It's okay." She jabbed at the shake with her straw, a clear signal that she didn't want to talk about it.

"Well, they say those things come in threes. Maybe you've filled your quota." Her glance flickered upward. He smiled, took a chance, and squeezed her hand to soften the joke. "And I promise to be careful around nail guns."

The gamble paid off. She laughed shakily. "The

point is, I've just learned it's better to count on myself."
No one to disappoint her. Or be disappointed in her.

"But you're pregnant. You're going to need help. You
can't do everything all by yourself." A rueful thought
occurred to him: *You sure didn't get pregnant all by
yourself.* Somehow, that obvious fact had escaped him
until now, and he found he didn't like the idea at all.
Thinking about how Meg had gotten pregnant by someone else.

"You mean you'd really do it?"

Craig blinked. He'd lost track of the conversation. He
didn't know what Meg was thinking of, but he was pretty
darned sure it wasn't the same thing he was. "Do what?"

She lowered her gaze and got very busy stirring her
shake with her straw. "What you said before." She raised
her eyes again. He'd never seen so much naked vulnera-
bility there. "Would you be my coach? Just for the class.
Lori promised she could make it for the delivery."

Craig swallowed hard. Somehow he'd talked his way
into being a temporary surrogate dad. "I said I would,
didn't I?"

"I'll help you finish decorating your mother's cabin."

He started to tell her that wasn't necessary, then decided it was better not to argue. He folded his arms and
smiled. "Deal."

Meg smiled back and felt a weight lift from her
shoulders. This was probably a really, really bad idea.
But somehow, she felt as if she'd done the right thing.

She reached across the table and picked up a French fry.

Just one.

"I appreciate this," Meg said again, a few nights later. She knew she was repeating herself, but it was something to say while they drove to class in Craig's truck. "It's really nice of you."

"No big deal," Craig said again.

He was being an awfully good sport about this. Still, Meg was worried. She doubted many husbands were all that comfortable in a Lamaze class, and Craig wasn't anybody's husband, least of all hers. She couldn't think of anyone else in Victory she'd feel more at ease with, but when it came to rehearsing for childbirth, that wasn't saying much. She wondered how Ron would have reacted to a class like this. Meg didn't know what to expect, herself.

The class met at a complex of medical office buildings across the street from the hospital. Upstairs. What sadist came up with that? Meg wondered as she trudged up the second half of the flight of stone steps, boosting her weight against the banister and trying to hide her breathlessness from Craig.

They traveled the walkway that wrapped around the outside of the building until they arrived at the right suite, and Craig pushed the door open for her.

Meg entered ahead of him and faced a relatively small room with a floor covered by mats. Pregnant women were scattered over about half of them, most of them with men sitting beside them.

"Where are the desks?" Craig said from behind her, and her heart sank.

She really, really hadn't expected to find herself sitting on the floor with Craig behind her, his long, denim-clad legs straddling either side of her. Meg wondered if Craig would believe that.

"Breathe in through your nose, out through your mouth," the maddeningly skinny blond instructor coached.

They were practicing the rapid breathing to use during a contraction. You were supposed to tighten your throat muscles and exhale with a hiss. Feeling like a fool, Meg complied, joining the chorus of hissing breaths around her.

She felt the warmth of Craig's body as he leaned closer to her ear and whispered, "It sounds like a roomful of spitting cobras."

Meg dissolved into giggles and earned herself a glare from the instructor.

That wasn't so bad. Then came the part where the men learned how to massage a woman's knotted muscles during childbirth. Craig complied without a word, working firm hands slowly from her lower back all the way up to her shoulders. Her muscles *were* tense. But Meg found the strength in Craig's touch anything but relaxing. She could picture his familiar rough hands as she felt the warm callouses on his fingers slowly knead the tender muscles at the base of her neck. Meg breathed deeply, as directed, but she knew her breaths shouldn't be coming this fast. She closed her eyes, grateful that Craig couldn't see the expression on her face.

"Easy," Craig murmured behind her. Two strong thumbs circled patiently, and Meg felt the tension begin to give way. Her resistance melted and her muscles relaxed under his hands. In response, he stroked her shoulders more broadly, squeezing them between his fingers and the heels of his hands. She was relaxed, but she missed the feel of his fingers against her skin. Almost involuntarily, she bent her head forward, hoping for his touch on her bare skin once again.

He didn't disappoint. Craig's hands worked their way back up without breaking contact, until his thumbs slid up to caress the sides of her neck. Meg drew in a long breath, trying her best to keep it silent.

"Here?" His voice was close to her ear.

She didn't want to speak, or nod, or do anything to interrupt. "Mmm," she volunteered reluctantly.

He continued his strokes, working his way up to the base of her scalp, discovering muscles Meg hadn't known needed massaging. She shuddered.

"Good or bad?" he murmured.

The instructor announced the class break, saving her

from having to reply. Meg was glad. If she'd had to answer him, it might have come out as a whimper.

During the break, pregnant women shuffled around and outside the room with cups of hot apple cider. Before Craig could ask where she wanted to go, Meg opted for the walkway outside the classroom, desperate for some space and fresh air.

Craig leaned back against the waist-high black metal rail and sipped his cider. In the chilly night air, thick clouds of steam rose from the styrofoam cup. "Don't you ever get cold?"

Meg realized she'd left her jacket inside, while Craig still wore his sleeveless ski vest over a long-sleeved shirt. She laughed. "Not much, any more. Pregnancy gives you a kind of built-in insulation." She glanced toward the door, wondering how long they had until it was time to go back in. "You know, Craig, you don't have to do this. I know it's not what you were expecting." *And I didn't picture sitting on the floor and getting massaged until I practically had to beg for mercy.*

He raised his eyebrows at her over the steam. "I told you, it's no big deal."

"I didn't really know what to expect either. I knew there were breathing exercises, but I didn't think . . ."

"Hey, I'll just look at it as a one-time experience. After all, I probably won't be doing it for any kids of my own." Meg felt a funny little lance through her chest.

He shrugged. "Who knows? Maybe I'll even write a book about it. You know, 'Handyman Takes Lesson in Baby Construction.' "

She frowned. "You're sure it's okay?"

"If it wasn't I'd say so." Craig took another sip. A wicked light came into his eyes. "You seem tense. You know, I noticed you have this tight little knot right here." He reached toward the place just between her neck and her left shoulder, raising memories of how he'd made the knot dissolve.

She backed away. Was he trying to break the tension or create more of it? Either way, his nearness made her heart hammer. She worked up a smile. "Save it for class, playboy."

Craig returned the smile and crushed his empty cup. "Suit yourself." He turned and walked back into the classroom ahead of her. Meg stayed behind to extend her reprieve for a few extra moments before going back inside. She'd been worried about how Craig would handle the course, but she seemed to be the only one who was having a problem. Craig was cool as a cucumber.

Craig was freezing.

When he got back inside, he asked the teacher about the room's extreme air conditioning in the middle of February. She explained that the classroom temperature was "mother controlled." Apparently pregnant women felt hot a lot, and since there was a limit to the amount of clothing they could take off, their partners were simply told to dress warmly. The rest of the class knew the rules by now, but not Craig. He rarely needed more than the ski vest, but next week he'd be sure to wear his heavy pullover.

It must be almost time to start class again. He searched for Meg. She stood across the room, talking to a young pregnant woman who'd come to class with an older woman, probably her mother. Craig remembered what she'd said before: *Find someone who's worse off than you are.*

He hadn't counted on the childbirth class putting him in such close quarters with his pregnant pal, but he wasn't about to let her know that. And he wasn't about to let her know how much it made him want to touch her again.

How long had he been kidding himself? He'd been fighting his attraction to Meg for weeks. Maybe ever since he met her at Mojave Burger, and he'd had plenty of warnings between now and then. Even that first flash of legs down the hall at the church should have warned him.

But this wasn't a flash of legs. This was Meg, his friend, who was having a *baby* in a few weeks, for crying out loud. Something he'd always been sure he'd never want. Meg, who made chocolate cake and threw snowballs and stole French fries when she didn't even know she was doing it. Meg, who vowed she didn't want to need anybody.

Well, that was good. If she broke his heart she probably wouldn't even notice.

* * *

No more massaging in the second half of class, much to Craig's relief. And disappointment. Instead, the instructor had the expectant mothers hold an ice cube in the palm of one hand while they practiced their breathing techniques. She called it physical rehearsal. It was supposed to be an exercise in pain management, to teach them how focusing could help alleviate the discomfort. Once again, hissing breaths filled the room.

"Okay, coaches," the instructor said, "it's your turn."

Meg relinquished the wet ice cube to Craig with a wry smile.

Definitely more than he'd bargained for.

Now the room filled with the sound of hissing males, and Craig was one of them. He felt like a buffoon, but at least he was one of about twelve buffoons. At first, the ice cube felt like no big deal. But over the course of thirty seconds, the ache spread through his hand, and it was hard to ignore. When the time was up, Craig was glad to dump the ice on the provided paper towel. Did labor contractions really last up to ninety seconds? He shook his aching hand.

"Yeah, right," a woman alongside him harrumphed. "That's *nothing.*"

He sensed Meg stiffen.

"When I have my baby," Meg said in the truck as Craig drove her home from class, "I'm *never* going to talk about labor in front of a pregnant woman."

"Of course not." Craig gave her shoulder a brief pat,

then removed his hand as if he were afraid of contracting typhoid fever. He was sending mixed signals tonight. During the class break, when he'd reached for her shoulder, she'd almost thought he was flirting with her. Would she ever get rid of these pregnancy-driven delusions?

Yes, in about four weeks. The hard way.

"Maybe labor stories are kind of like war stories for men," he said. "After all, women don't get battle scars."

"Just stretch marks."

Craig cast her a sidelong glance, and Meg felt herself blush in the cab of the pickup. Or maybe the warmth in her face came from the heater, which he had cranked up unusually high. So far, she didn't have any stretch marks—she'd been slathering her growing girth with lotion in an attempt to prevent it—but there was no point mentioning that to Craig.

"You'll do fine," he said. Everyone said that, Meg noticed—when they weren't busy telling horror stories. "Said any prayers lately?"

She wouldn't have expected him to remember the story she'd told him about her prayer, back on the day he'd built the diaper table. "As a matter of fact, I did," Meg said. "Heard a voice, too."

"Oh? What'd it say?"

She grinned. " 'You fool! Don't you know what you're getting into?!' "

They both laughed. Unorthodox as this was, Meg was still glad she'd chosen Craig over Helen. She shifted her hand on her stomach, reminding herself again what this was all about. Jimmy would be worth it. She closed her eyes and tried to use a trick from the Lamaze class: concentrate on a focal point. She pictured a perfect baby boy, sleeping serenely in the white wicker bassinet she'd set up by her side of the bed at home. His face was smooth and peaceful, even prettier than Lori's baby. She inhaled deeply, imagining the soft sound of her baby's breathing.

Craig pulled away from a stop, and her head bobbed forward. The image dissolved. Eyes still closed, Meg tried again, but the heat inside the truck made it hard to concentrate. This time, try as she might, her mind insisted on conjuring up a pair of teasing blue eyes. She studied them, trying to read what was behind the teasing, but she couldn't decipher it. Then she became aware he was holding something, and looked down to see a blanket-wrapped bundle in his arms.

The truck jerked again, and she opened her eyes with a start. Somehow, they'd already reached her apartment. And she'd slumped over, her head resting on something warm and firm. Meg shifted her heavy head, and her face brushed Craig's shoulder.

"Hey." Craig's voice was soft as he joggled his shoulder slightly under her cheek. "You fell asleep."

A streetlight illuminated his face, so much like the image she'd dreamed, but the teasing expression was gone. Instead, his eyes had a gentle look she'd never seen before. Of course, she'd never seen them this close up before.

"Sorry." Meg tried to shake off the languid feeling that had settled into her limbs. Her voice felt thick. "It's past my bedtime."

"Nine-thirty?" A little amusement crept back into his eyes, but the gentleness didn't leave. He was so close. It would be so easy to reach up, just to touch that thick swatch of hair that fell over his forehead. What would he do if she did? She almost had the feeling he wanted her to. To pull his head down to hers . . .

Meg opened her door to let in a blast of cold air.

And waited, dutifully, for Craig to come around and help her down.

Craig walked her to the door; at least there were no stairs here. Meg slid her key into the lock. "Do you want a cup of coffee or anything?" She wasn't sure if she ought to offer, or whether or not she wanted him to say yes. The way her mind was working right now, she might say or do something really idiotic.

"Uh, no, thanks." Craig backed away as she turned for his answer. "See you next week."

Craig bolted to his truck, gunned it, and was speeding away by the time she got her door open. No, he definitely didn't want to hang around for coffee.

Chapter Eight

Craig flipped the switch and waited to see if the lights overhead exploded in a shower of sparks. Instead, they flickered briefly, then illuminated the first half of the long church corridor.

He turned to his friend Steve. "Thanks, man. You did it without blowing the place up."

"Told you so." Steve dusted off his hands on his jeans. "I can finish the other half of the hallway before we knock off, if you want."

Craig glanced at his watch. In about half an hour, he'd need to call it a day, go home, and change before he picked up Meg for Lamaze class tonight. "No, let's start that part tomorrow."

He hadn't seen Meg in the week since the first class, but that hadn't stopped him from thinking about her. A really bad sign. And suddenly, Victory seemed to suffer from an epidemic of pregnant women and babies. He saw them everywhere he went, even Home Depot, where by rights it should have been safe. There was no escape. He supposed they'd been there all along, but he'd never noticed.

That reminded him of something. "Hey, Steve, did your wife have that baby yet?"

Steve glanced up from gathering his equipment. "Are you kidding? Try five months ago."

"Oh." He *really* hadn't been paying attention before. Steve was one of the few friends from Craig's high school shop class he'd stayed in touch with. Steve's face looked just a little fuller, his waist just a little wider, than Craig remembered from those days. Like Craig, Steve had opted to make a living working with his hands and staying out of trouble. Unlike Craig, he specialized in electrical work, which came in handy when he needed someone to rewire ancient buildings. "Guess I haven't seen you for longer than I thought."

"Think time flies now? Wait till you have kids." Steve shook his head. "She's growing up so fast. She rolled over for the first time the other day."

Roll over? It sounded like something dogs were supposed to do. But Steve seemed proud, so it must be a good thing. "That's great."

"You should come over some time for dinner."

Craig hesitated. He supposed it was time he got together with friends for something other than work. He usually avoided family situations, but those strained dinners at home when he was a teenager were a long time ago now. Time to shake off those bad associations. "Sure."

"How about—"

The high-pitched buzz of Craig's cell phone interrupted. He pulled it off his belt. "Stovall Construction."

"Craig?" A female voice came in through a crackle of static. The reception in this building, with the church's thick walls and high roof, was miserable. "It's Meg." The cell phone cut out little pieces of her words. "I've got to—" The rest was lost.

"Meg? You're breaking up."

"So are you. I'll talk fast. I'm at the hospital. I—"

"Hospital?" Craig interrupted, cutting into vital connection seconds. He started down the hall toward the exit so he could get outside these walls and hear more clearly. Instead, his movement got him a dead silence, and for an instant he thought he'd lost her completely. He stopped halfway down the hall, turned slowly, and was rewarded by the return of crackling air.

". . . okay?" Meg faded back in. "You can meet me . . ." and her voice crackled away again.

Craig's insides clenched. Meg, at the hospital. Labor, or something worse? And where was Lori? That's right, this was Wednesday, the night she had that stupid seminar, which was why he was in this spot in the first place.

"I'll be there," he said loudly into the cell phone. Nothing but dead silence on the other end. He'd lost the connection for sure. He snapped the phone shut and turned to Steve. "I have to go." He cast a helpless eye at the hallway around him, strewn with tools and light fixtures. "A friend of mine's at the hospital. I think she's in labor. Can you and Lance lock up? He's got a set of keys."

Steve waved him away. "Go. We'll handle it."

As Craig vaulted down the hall, Steve called after him, "It might just be Braxton Hicks."

"Thanks." Craig rounded the corner for the exit.

Who the heck was Braxton Hicks?

"Megan Reilly," Craig repeated to the heavy, red-haired woman behind the circular counter in Labor and Delivery. "She called me from here. She would have checked in, probably in the last hour or so."

The annoyingly placid woman consulted a mysterious binder and shook her head. "We haven't had anyone check in since ten-thirty this morning."

Could she have been here that long before she called anyone? "What's the name?"

"I'm sorry, I can't release—"

An infant's loud squall rang out from the hallway behind him. It sounded like a swarm of angry bees. Craig swung around toward the sound and saw Meg.

She stood halfway down the corridor from the reception area, a blanket-wrapped bundle on her shoulder. But her stomach, in profile as she swayed her body trying to quiet the screaming bundle, was every bit as round as before. For a split second Craig wondered how she was able to balance the extra weight, the one around her middle and the one on her shoulder, so gracefully. Then he reached her in several long strides.

Meg turned, eyes wide. "What are you doing here?"

Craig stared at her. "You're still pregnant."

Meg stared back. *Well, of course,* she almost said, but a second glance at Craig's glazed eyes and tousled hair stopped her. From the look of things, their cell phone conversation had been more garbled than she thought. He'd arrived here in a panic. Had he been worried about her? The thought gave her a flicker of warmth before Jackie's baby let out another cry right next to her ear, calling her back to the present.

She patted his little soft back, wishing she could find some magic maneuver that would calm him down. Jackie didn't need to hear her baby cry, not on top of everything else. She walked a little farther from the doorway of Jackie's room, still twisting and bobbing to appease the infant. At the end of the hall, the nurse behind the counter eyed her watchfully, probably on the alert for psycho pregnant women trying to make off with other people's babies.

Her attention returned to the dazed look on Craig's face. "I'm okay," she said when the baby paused for a gulp of air. "Jackie had her baby today. She's one of the girls from the Joshua Center." She tried a circular rubbing motion on the baby's back, and the wailing paused, at least momentarily. "She called me at work." Meg tried to ease the baby down a little lower on her shoulder, away from her ear. Any lower and he might start trying to nurse, the way he had with Jackie a little while ago. No point in Craig seeing that; he was already staring at the little bundle as if it were a live cobra.

"So why'd you call me?"

A little blunt, but maybe he was still shell-shocked. "To tell you to meet me at class tonight. I wasn't sure I'd get home in time for you to pick me up."

"Oh." Craig's shoulders, always so broad and solid, went a little slack.

He *had* been worried about her. It was there in the weariness of his eyes, the slump of his shoulders. And he'd been there for her at a moment's notice. Meg's throat tightened. "I'm sorry. I didn't mean to make you run down here. I guess you couldn't hear me. But— thanks." She slowed her circles on the baby's cotton-clad back, gratified when he stayed quiet. Meg felt a surge of tenderness, whether from Craig's presence or the intimate warmth of the baby in her arms, she wasn't sure. Impulsively she stepped forward. "Want a closer look?"

He didn't quite step back, but he flinched visibly. "No, that's okay."

A sharp sting hit Meg; she tried to ignore it. She couldn't let her emotions run away with her, not now. Just holding the baby had every hormone in her body singing a jangling, discordant melody. But this wasn't about her. She swallowed hard and backed away. "I'd better get back to Jackie."

Inside the room, Jackie was propped up in the bed,

half-sitting, half-lying. Her friend Britney, who'd been Jackie's labor coach, hovered near the head of the bed like a bodyguard in black eyeliner. No sign of the father, of course.

Meg kept up her circles on the little boy's back, afraid he'd start crying again if she stopped. "He seems to like this," she said, looking from one girl to the other. She wasn't sure if Jackie would want to try holding him again. The teen's eyes were still red-rimmed. Britney stepped forward and accepted the baby. Miraculously, he stayed quiet.

Meg bent down to hug Jackie. "It'll be okay," she said. The girl's shoulders trembled under her loose blue hospital gown.

The room darkened ever so slightly. Meg straightened to see Craig's figure hovering in the doorway. She shook her head, hoping Craig would see the gesture from across the room. Jackie didn't need unfamiliar visitors, not now. Craig hung back, whether because he'd seen her or because of his own discomfort, Meg couldn't tell.

"He's beautiful, isn't he?" Jackie murmured.

It might have been the sound of Jackie's voice; suddenly, the baby reared his head back under Britney's hand, then launched himself at her shoulder as if he'd batter his way in to wherever the milk was.

"I don't think that first bottle was enough for him," Meg said. That was an understatement. "Want me to go down to the nurse's station and get another one?"

"I'll do it," Britney said.

"Thanks." Meg met the girl's eyes as she passed and gave her a nod of appreciation. Silence followed after she left.

"You don't have to stay," Jackie said. Her voice quavered a little. "I just wanted you to see him."

"I'm so glad you called me." Meg worked hard to keep her own voice steady, and gave Jackie's hand a squeeze. If Jackie was anything like her, another hug might set off a fresh spate of tears. "And I'm proud of you."

"Really?"

"Really." Meg smiled. "You're sure you don't need anything while I'm here?"

"No." A weak smile. "Britney's got me covered."

Meg nodded. Britney was being fiercely territorial, but the girl seemed to have Jackie's best interest at heart, and not just excitement over the novelty of a friend who'd given birth. Meg waited until Britney returned with baby and bottle, and left before she lost her own composure.

Craig was waiting in the hallway. He looked incongruous, leaning against the maternity wing's peach wall in a dusty navy sweatshirt. The sight brought out a huge bundle of conflicting emotions Meg didn't want to examine long enough to name. Lamaze class started in about half an hour; she'd have to keep those feelings in check. Holding Jackie's baby had stirred up enough emotions in her already.

He didn't even want to look at the baby. It was an irrational thought and she knew it. Why would Craig be interested in anyone's baby, let alone a stranger's? She started down the hall beside him, not meeting his eyes. "Thanks for coming," she said.

"Sure." She sensed him trying to peer at her face. "When you called I really thought—"

"You must have been relieved." *If I'd had the baby you might have actually had to touch it or something.*

"Well, yeah. You're not due for, what is it, another month?"

"Three weeks." Meg bit her lip.

The hospital had turned into a nonsensical maze of corridors. Meg couldn't recall for the life of her how she'd reached the labor and delivery wing, let alone Jackie's room. They came to a wall at the end of a hallway; it branched off in opposite directions. Meg stopped. Right or left? She couldn't remember. As she debated, Craig took her arm and started to steer her gently to the right. Meg turned, but didn't walk.

"She decided to give the baby up for adoption," she said.

"Oh." Craig paused, his hand still hovering at her elbow. His blue eyes scoured her face. At times, it felt as if he could see right into her, but now, it felt more like he was trying to read tea leaves. "That's a good thing, isn't it?"

"I think it's the best thing for both of them. She's sixteen, she doesn't make any money, she doesn't have any support from her family. . . ."

She wondered if Craig would see the obvious parallels to her own situation. If he did, he didn't comment.

"On your hands and knees, moms," the blond instructor chirped. If it was possible, she'd managed to get more insanely chipper in the past week. "Now rock back and forth. This can ease your contractions. . . ."

Meg crouched on her hands and knees in a rough imitation of a cow standing in a field, while Craig hovered alongside her. She bent her head down, letting her hair fall forward to hide her face. Last week, there would have been a fifty-fifty chance she'd start giggling uncontrollably. But tonight she was far from a giggling mood.

They'd driven to class from the hospital in their separate vehicles, sparing Meg the prospect of more conversation. In her state of mind, she might have said any number of stupid things.

She'd been testing Craig, she realized, throwing someone else's baby up to him and expecting him to react. When she knew all along how he'd react. He'd been up front with her from the beginning. He wasn't interested in children. When had she started deluding herself that he might change his mind? And why did she want him to? Just because he was a big, strong male? Or because he was Craig?

If it was just because she wanted a big, strong man, someone to take care of her again, she should be ashamed of herself. If it was because he was Craig, she was in even bigger trouble.

The class moved on to breathing exercises. Meg leaned back against Craig as instructed, using him as a sort of human chair and trying hard not to notice how warm and firm he felt behind her. How good it felt to lean against him.

He wouldn't look at the baby. That shouldn't matter to her. She couldn't afford any insane daydreams. She didn't want, didn't need, anyone big and strong to come along and save her. She knew better. She'd been prepared, from the outset, to be both mother and father to her little boy.

"Breathe," the teacher instructed, and Meg complied. Inside her stomach, Jimmy reacted to the influx of oxygen with a huge flip-flop. He must be doing somersaults in there.

And Craig's hands, resting at the sides of her stomach, jerked sharply. A natural enough reaction—especially from a single guy feeling a baby that wasn't his.

She was alone in this, completely on her own. Well, what did she expect? When, in all the time since she'd gotten the news of Ron's death, had she ever expected anything else? But she'd forgotten something in the equation. Memories of Jackie's little boy swam in front of her, unbidden.

Find someone who's worse off than you. She'd tried to follow that advice, believing that God had put the

words into her head. Maybe he had. She'd found someone worse off than herself, all right.

Jimmy.

Meg said very little during class, so Craig followed
suit. When a woman was that quiet, it usually meant
she was shy, depressed, or wanted to bite your head off.
He didn't want to find out which one during class. If it
was something he'd done, he'd know soon enough. But
as soon as the teacher dismissed them, Meg gave him a
small smile, said "See you next week," and made
straight for the door.

What was that all about? All of a sudden she couldn't
walk to the parking lot with him?

He could have left her alone, but that would be the
coward's way out. By now he'd been around Meg enough
to know something was wrong. So, invited or not, he
trailed after her as she walked outside. "Hey, wait."

She turned back to him with the same fixed smile. "I
have to go." The rest of the class bustled past them to
the stairs.

"Or what? You'll turn into a pumpkin? Come on,
you've hardly said a word all night. What's up?"

The halfhearted smile disappeared. Craig tried to
make out Meg's expression by the security lights outside the building. The lighting wasn't quite enough to
read her face. It did illuminate the soft line of her
cheek, and the hint of shadows under her eyes.

Behind them, the instructor locked the classroom door and wished them a cheery good night. Then they were alone.

Tonight it was even colder than last week, the air brittle around them. In all the chaos, Craig hadn't had a chance to get home and change into that pullover he'd promised himself last week. In fact, he hadn't even grabbed his ski vest when he bolted out of the church, leaving him in his sweatshirt from work. He held his elbows close to his body, grateful that the air was still. If any wind came up, it would be brutal.

Meg's silence had stretched on for a long time. Maybe he should have let her go and left well enough alone. But if she wanted to bite his head off, he figured she would have done it by now. "Talk to me, Meg. What is it?"

She let out a long breath and turned away, gripping the railing of the upper level walkway. Craig took a spot beside her and leaned over the cold rail for a glimpse of her profile. With her back to the building, Meg's features were even harder to make out. She stared straight ahead, somewhere far beyond the view of the parking lot.

At last she spoke. "Maybe I shouldn't be doing this."

"Doing what?"

"The baby." He recognized the flat, controlled voice of the woman from the confessional. "Jackie's giving her baby up for adoption. Maybe I should be doing the same thing."

He couldn't have been more surprised if she'd told him she was joining a Satanic cult. "You're kidding."

Her eyes remained straight ahead.

She was serious. A strange sensation, almost like horror, twisted in the pit of Craig's stomach. Meg give up her baby? He was amazed at how wrong it sounded. "Meg, you already love that baby more than . . . more than I loved my first car."

The feeble joke didn't go over. "I know. That's why I should want what's best for him." She raised a finger to the corner of her eye, wiping at something Craig couldn't see. "He's kept me going all this time. But maybe I'm just being selfish. You were right. A baby really should grow up with two parents."

"I never said you should give the baby up."

"I didn't say it to Jackie either."

"It's not the same thing. You're not some teen mother."

"How different am I? Really?"

Craig opened his mouth to argue, then saw Meg's line of thinking. No husband. No family. And as the assistant manager at a clothing store in Victory, probably not much money.

How had his mother managed? The money would have been tight—he could remember stretches where she'd juggled two jobs—but coping with Craig on her own must have been even harder. He couldn't think of a thing she should have done differently, and he'd still given her the devil's own time of it. All the time when he was out making trouble, he knew now, he'd just been begging for someone to stop him. The right someone.

The phantom father, whom he still knew practically nothing about.

He bit his tongue before something stupid came out of his mouth. Something like, *I'll help you.* Because, what could he possibly do?

Meg's voice remained dull and matter-of-fact. "I don't make much money. He'll grow up in a little apartment, I'll have to leave him in day care all day . . ." She sniffled a little. "And I can't even throw a baseball."

I can throw a baseball.

Craig tried to picture himself playing catch with a little boy. How old were kids when they learned to throw, anyway? One, three, five? But Meg didn't need a friend to help out for a little while now and then. Not some eternal Uncle Craig, dropping by to play catch once a week, assuming this tentative friendship held out. She needed someone for overnight feedings. To help change diapers. All the other millions of things babies needed, that Craig didn't know a thing about. She needed someone for the long haul. And she didn't deserve any less.

Craig couldn't afford to say anything he didn't mean, make any promises he couldn't keep. But he couldn't stand to hear Meg talk this way, either. "Meg, I know how much you want this baby." He leaned farther over the rail, trying to get her to look at him. "No one else could love him like you do."

"I don't know if that's enough."

He studied the side of her face. The half-light couldn't

hide the set of her chin, that look of determination even as she contemplated the unthinkable. Craig sucked in his breath, reached for her shoulders, and turned her to face him. One look at Meg and he needed another breath. Her dark eyes wavered somewhere between desperation and hope, and still she gazed back at him without looking away. Her shoulders took on a firmer set under his hands. Even now, she wasn't asking for help.

Some strong feeling welled up inside him, more powerful than any Good Samaritan impulse. He didn't just want to help Meg. He didn't just admire her stubborn insistence on taking care of herself. It was some lethal combination of the two that shook him to the core.

Run, he thought. *Run before you get in any deeper.*

Run? He couldn't even move. Maybe it was because it was so cold.

Don't say anything you don't mean. Don't say anything you can't take back.

He drew in one more breath and said the truest thing he could think of. "Meg, *you're* what's best for your baby." He held her with his eyes. She had to believe him. "You can't keep your hands off your own stomach. You've got a nursery full of farm animals. You're going to be out there making snowmen in the yard with him." Suddenly it was hard for him to speak. "Jimmy's *lucky* to have you for a mother."

A little of the stiffness left her shoulders, and the desperation in her eyes faded. He was sure of it. For once, he'd managed to say the right thing.

He squeezed her shoulders. "So no more crazy talk, okay?"

He didn't want to let go until he heard the right answer. Maybe he didn't want to let go at all.

Meg closed her eyes and let out a sigh. "Okay." Her voice was half a whisper.

Her shoulders relaxed. Craig imagined he could literally feel a weight falling away from them. Something inside him relaxed, too. Why Meg's decision was so important to him, he didn't know. Or didn't want to know.

She opened her eyes, and her lips curved up slowly in a smile.

Unlike the one she'd given him on her way out the door, this one was real. It filled him with an intoxicating warmth. Her eyes were soft, her face luminous, as if she were seeing the dawn after a long dark night. It was more than Craig could resist. Before he could think, before he could stop himself, he lowered his head toward hers.

And she laughed.

Inches from her mouth, Craig stopped, puzzled. Then she brushed at a fat snowflake on her cheek, and he understood. He followed her gaze upward and saw the tiny, scattered flakes from a late-winter Victory snowfall. They stood out against the dark sky, falling in windy trails around them.

Eyes still raised toward the sky, Meg stepped back and extended her arms, trying to catch more of the snowflakes. A moment later, she brought back an arm, triumphant. She'd captured a tiny crystal flake on the sleeve of her red jacket.

"Look." She crooked her arm upward for him to see. "You can see the pattern. It's true what they say. They really are all different."

Reluctantly, Craig dragged his eyes away from Meg to study the melting snowflake. It turned into a clear puddle on her jacket sleeve, then it soaked into the fabric, but another one landed nearby to take its place. She was right; Craig made out an intricate, crystalline pattern before it, too, dissolved. His gaze went back to her face. She was more beautiful than he'd ever seen her, with snowflakes clinging to her dark hair and a light of fresh hope in her eyes. One look at her and Craig did what he'd meant to do in the first place: He cupped her face in his hands and kissed her.

For a moment she stiffened. But only for a moment. Then there was a wonderful softness as her mouth yielded to his. Craig yielded too, giving himself up to the sensation of sinking in, being lost in her warmth. Slowly, he slid one hand around the back of her head, tangling his fingers in those rich, dark waves.

I can't, Meg thought. But she couldn't pull away from his gentle mouth, such a contrast to the firm palm that still rested against her cheek. Her lips parted, and Craig took it for the invitation it was, deepening the kiss until it felt as if they were completely joined. He reached around the small of her back, drawing her closer, as if to include the baby in their embrace.

When he lifted his mouth from hers, she started to protest, not wanting it to be over, but instead of drawing away, he nibbled lightly, teasingly, across her lower lip. She sighed against his mouth, and that was all the encouragement it took for him to kiss her again. This time she was waiting for him with a passion she'd forgotten existed. If it ever had. Meg pressed closer. She couldn't remember anything like this with Ron, this need to melt into him until everything else was gone.

And everything else did disappear, until his lips left hers. Meg didn't want to move. After a moment, with some difficulty, she opened her eyes, a little surprised to find herself still on the walkway outside the classroom. These past few minutes, she could have been on the moon and not known it. She realized dimly that the little flurry of snow had stopped, and the world around them had gotten very silent.

Craig loosened his hold, drawing back just enough to fill her eyes with his gaze. If it hadn't been for his arms around her, Meg didn't think she would have been able to stand up. The depth of feeling she saw in that gaze was so strong, so unreserved, it was almost more than she could handle. In those eyes, in that moment, she felt sure she saw someone who would always be there for her.

It took Jimmy to wake her up. He stirred inside her, as if he'd been wakened by the loud thumping of her heart.

Reflexively, Meg put her hand to the spot on her

stomach where she'd felt the baby squirm, to let him know his mother was still here.

She'd forgotten everything. Now they were back in the real world, a world where she couldn't afford to need anyone again, not this way. It wasn't worth the risk. She'd decided that months ago, after Ron's death, when she discovered just how dependent she'd let herself become. Meg had to survive on her own. How could she risk getting involved with someone who didn't even want a baby?

I can't.

She drew in a breath. It was hard to find her voice. "Why did you do that?"

Craig's hands dropped away from her. "Oh, I don't know, Meg. Why do you think?" He turned away, jamming his hands into his pockets.

Meg stared at Craig's back. A faint, chilly breeze slapped her face, when just a moment ago she'd felt so warm. She stepped up to Craig and tried to hook her hand through his upper arm. The muscles under his sweatshirt sleeve were hard and tense. "Craig, I'm sorry." She licked her lips, still moist from his kisses, and tried to think of a way to repair the damage. Only one excuse came to mind. "It's just—too soon."

He spun around to face her with surprising speed, and her hand fell away.

The anger in his eyes surprised her. "Come off it, Meg."

"What?" Her throat threatened to close up.

"Don't lie to me." He passed a hand roughly through his hair. "Slap my face or tell me to get lost, but don't lie to me."

The tightness in her throat grew. "What are you talking about?"

His eyes fixed on hers. "I know how you felt about your husband, Meg. That was no priest in the confessional that day. It was me."

Meg stared back at him, baffled. The confessional? Her mind jumped back a month. Then her eyes widened.

It was impossible. But how else would he know anything about her trip to the church? The cold from outside settled into the pit of her stomach. "I don't understand. How could you—"

"I was making repairs there."

Comprehension hit her full force. He'd heard everything she said that day, when she'd thought she was talking to a priest. Her mind raced, trying to remember it all. Everything Craig had known about her, all this time. He knew about the fight with Ron. That Ron hadn't wanted a baby.

That she wasn't sure she loved her husband.

He knew she was a fraud. She felt stripped, exposed.

Meg gulped in a breath. She could only think of one thing to do.

Run.

She went for the stone steps, holding tight to the rail and taking them as fast as she could.

"Meg." Craig's voice was close behind her, his heavier footsteps reverberating on the stairs. She didn't slow down.

"Meg, wait." His voice was insistent. She'd almost reached the landing that divided the stairs in half.

Craig vaulted past and hit the landing before her. His arms stretched across both sides of the railing, blocking her way.

"Meg," he said, *"the baby."*

Eight months pregnant, and she was running down stairs. Meg froze.

One of the lights overhead illuminated Craig's face as he looked up at her. The anger was gone. His blue eyes were full of naked concern, and maybe that was even worse.

She couldn't face him. But there was only one place to hide.

Meg moved forward, buried her face in the front of his sweatshirt, and cried.

Chapter Nine

She was trapped.

Craig's arms surrounded Meg while she cried. It was comforting for the moment, but she knew the brief warmth and safety came with a price. She had to pull away eventually, and she didn't want to look at him. Not now. He'd known all about her, all along, and he'd never told her. He'd gotten involved in her life, let her trust him. Why?

As soon as her sobs ran out, Meg clenched her hands and pushed back, keeping her eyes away from his face. Instead, she stared resolutely at his sweatshirt and wondered why he wasn't wearing something warmer. She shook the thought off. So what if he was cold?

She should just get away, but she needed answers. "What's going on? Is this all some kind of joke?"

"No. It was an accident."

"An accident?" She stepped the rest of the way back from his arms. Craig moved forward, his hand hovering

146

near her elbow. Meg glanced down and remembered that they still stood on the landing of the stone stairway, its surface wet from the snow. She pulled her arm away and gripped the waist-high rail surrounding the outer edge. "Then how'd you track me down at Mojave Burger?"

"An accident," Craig repeated. "I recognized your jacket. I saw it when you left the church."

"I don't believe you."

"It's the truth."

"You sat there and listened—"

"It happened too fast. I didn't know how to stop you."

She'd been in a hurry to unload, all right—when she thought it was anonymous. A new wave of humiliation hit her. "You knew all those things, all this time, and you never told me?"

"How could I?" He rested a hand on the railing between her and the rest of the stairs, blocking her escape route. "What would you have done?"

Before she could think, Meg met his eyes. Big mistake. Craig's stare held her pinned, as surely as his arm blocked her way.

No wonder he'd always seemed to understand her so well. It had all been a lie, a cheat. And if she didn't get out of here fast, he might get to see her fall apart again. She wouldn't let that happen. She tried to push his arm out of her way, but it held rigid, his muscles rock steady.

"I'm sorry," he said. "I should have told you. But—I

don't know, I just dug myself into a hole. And the longer I knew you, the deeper it got."

She never should have looked at him. Meg struggled for breath. Even in the half-light, she felt naked under his eyes. Her mouth went dry. "Let me go."

"Not until you hear me out." How could he be so calm? "I said I was sorry, Meg. Now I want you to listen to me."

She didn't have much choice. She couldn't shove her way past the strength of his arm, and now she couldn't seem to tear away from the persistence of his gaze.

"Think about it," he said. "I've spent the last two Wednesday nights in a room full of panting pregnant women. I dropped everything and *ran* to the hospital tonight when you called, because I thought you were in labor. Why would I do that?"

She hesitated. "You must have a sick sense of humor."

"Uh-uh." His free hand touched the side of her face, and Meg's knees wobbled. If there was one thing she wasn't prepared to handle, it was a caress.

"What I still don't understand," Craig said, "is what's so terrible."

"About what? About having someone know all the worst things about you?"

He actually smiled. "I think two-thirds of this town knows the worst things about me."

"That's different. Things like speeding tickets—"

"And shoplifting."

"You were a kid."

"What's the difference? You think God forgives everyone but you?"

Meg drew in a breath. That struck dangerously close to home.

Craig lightly traced the bottom of her chin with his thumb. Meg gripped the rail tighter. The feeling that made her knees quiver now wasn't just anger, or fear, or tension. It was the memory, so recent, of his lips on hers.

"What I meant was," Craig said, his voice very low, "I don't understand what was so horrible about what you told me. Maybe you made a mistake when you got married. Maybe you weren't really in love the way you thought you were. But it doesn't make you an ax murderer."

"I'm a fraud." She spat the words out with as much force as she could. "A fake. A phony."

"No, you're not." The base of his thumb was firm and calloused under her chin, but his touch was soft. It made her want him to touch her more. She couldn't let him know that. "If you were fooling Ron, you were fooling yourself, too. I know you, Meg. You're a good person. Probably the nicest person I've ever met. You need to stop being so hard on yourself."

There it was again. The priest's advice, in that same comforting voice. Meg was amazed she'd never recognized it before. And for a moment, with Craig looking down at her, she was tempted to believe it again. She couldn't seem to look away from his eyes. They were too close, too direct, and there was something dangerously tender in them. He knew all about her, and still he looked at her that way.

The cold breeze blew harder, tempting her to huddle close to him. Warmth and support were so near, yet so far.

"So why'd you do all this?" Her voice came out a whisper.

He gave a deep, ragged sigh. "You haven't figured it out by now? I thought *I* was slow."

Craig's thumb caressed the delicate skin along her jaw line, bringing back memories of the embrace they'd shared just a little while ago. He wouldn't dare kiss her again. Would he?

If he did, would she be able to make herself stop him?

Once again, Jimmy intervened. He hiccupped, startling Meg out of the near-hypnotic spell she'd begun to fall under. She held her hand to the spot where she'd felt the little jouncing sensation.

Craig's eyes followed her hand. "Is something wrong?"

"No. The baby has the hiccups."

"They do that?" She nodded. Then Craig did something she'd never expected. He placed a hand next to hers, on her belly.

After a moment her stomach jumped again. "Wow," he said. His hand twitched, but this time he didn't lift it away. It was the first time she'd seen him react to a baby without pulling back. Was she imagining the wonder on his face?

Meg ventured to put a hand over his, and still Craig showed no inclination to pull away. She stared down at their hands as they rested together on her stomach. She thought of the way he'd held her earlier, with Jimmy nestled between them. It was so quiet she could hear the almost inaudible sound of dripping around them, as the tiny snowflakes returned to their liquid state and dripped from the overhang of the building.

"You *are* keeping this guy, right?" Craig said. His voice was quiet, as if he didn't want to drown out the dripping of the snow.

She nodded.

"I'm glad," he said.

Craig waited, and after a moment, it came again— that tiny jolt from inside Meg's stomach. His pulse sped up with some unnamable reaction. He wasn't sure what he felt—a cross between fascination and alarm. There was someone *alive* in there. He'd known it intellectually, but somehow it had never really hit him until now.

She looked up at him then, and the softness he saw in her face caught him completely off guard. Craig knew he was seeing the real Meg, without any defenses, and maybe for the first time. His heart hammered. A while ago he'd been trying not to kiss her. Now he was hit by a feeling so intense he was afraid if he opened his mouth, he'd promise her everything. The moon, the stars, the next fifty years of his life.

Craig took a deep breath and silently counted to ten. "So, where do we go from here?"

Meg sighed, and something seemed to drain out of her. "There's nowhere *to* go."

"I thought we were past that. I understand about Ron. Can't we just be honest with each other now?"

In a way, having her know the truth about that day in the confessional was a relief. No more need to watch what he said, pretending he believed things were one way when he knew they were another. And after all this, there wasn't much point in pretending he didn't care about Meg. Not to himself, and not to her.

"It's not just Ron," she said. "I told you before, I need to be on my own. When Ron died I made myself a promise. I never want to need anybody again. The only person I want to count on is me."

"I don't know, Meg. It seems like a funny way to bring up a baby. Is that how you're going to raise Jimmy? Not to need anyone? To be an island?"

"That's different."

"It's always different when it's someone else, isn't it?" Meg's thinking was starting to make a baffling kind of sense to him. "You've got some of the weirdest double standards I've ever seen. It's okay for other people to make mistakes, but not you. It's okay for that girl Jackie to need you, or your baby to need you, but you're not allowed to need anyone else. What's wrong with letting someone be there for you, for a change?"

She wet her lips. "You couldn't cope with a baby. You said so yourself."

This was going *way* too fast. "Wait a minute. I didn't

say I was building any picket fences yet. Can't we just take it from here, one step at a time?"

"There's no point. Why get hurt more, later on?"

"Meg, if you want a guarantee that nothing else is ever going to go wrong, you're going to be disappointed."

"I know." Her voice was hollow again. "People get killed. People leave."

"Well, I can't promise I'll never get killed. But if you can't trust me a little by now—"

Her lips quirked up in an ironic smile. "Trust?"

Craig's heart fell. They were back where they'd started. He should have known it all along. She'd put up one barrier after another, and it was a waste of time wondering which one was the bottom line. A woman with that many barriers didn't want him in.

Craig sighed. "Look, Meg," he said, "I've done all I can. I've been as honest as I know how to be. And I want the best for you. I really do." The cold wind cut through his sweatshirt, clear to his skin.

He looked into her eyes and said softly, with regret, "But I think you'd better find another Lamaze partner."

Chapter Ten

Salsa. That was the ticket. Meg spooned a big dollop onto her plate, alongside the cream cheese, and dipped her cracker into both.

"Won't that give you heartburn?" Annette, one of Lori's friends, looked on dubiously.

Meg managed a wry grin. "I don't think it makes much difference. I already sleep sitting up with three pillows every night as it is."

A general, empathetic chuckle went up around her. Out of all five women at Lori's scrapbooking get-together, Meg was the only one who hadn't had a baby yet.

As they settled around Lori's long dining room table to start working on their photo albums, girl talk bubbled up from all sides.

"I remember with my first, I could eat *anything*. Then with my daughter, everything set my stomach off."

"I was always dying for chocolate."

"Strawberries."

"Mexican food," Meg chimed in. Since she hadn't seen Craig in several days, her fast food consumption was way down. But she found herself concocting her own homemade burritos and tacos, with generous dollops of guacamole and sour cream, after she eased her conscience first with some fresh fruit or vegetables.

Yes, she'd eaten a *lot* these past several days.

"There's your trouble," Annette said. "Salsa, pickles, even milk—they all make heartburn worse when you're pregnant. But it helps if you don't eat for about two hours before you go to bed. . . ."

Meg soaked in the chatter, content to listen and offer the occasional comment, just as long as they didn't start on labor stories. Coming to Lori's tonight had been a good idea. She'd fought her way through a thick layer of depression and burritos to get here, but in the days since she last saw Craig, she'd come to a realization. She'd made a mistake, trying so hard to be independent that she'd isolated herself. Craig was right about that much; no one was an island. And if she relaxed enough to open up to more people, she'd be less likely to fall into the trap of depending on a man again.

She'd set herself up to be vulnerable, she realized. To Craig, of all people—the one person who'd known enough about her to make a fortune in blackmail before they even met.

While they talked, Meg sorted through the photographs she'd brought. At first the idea of a decorative photo album had sounded hokey, just a pleasant way to pry herself out of her empty apartment for some much-needed social contact. But after Lori's little semi-rehearsed presentation at the beginning of the evening, Meg found she liked the idea of using colored paper and pens to highlight pictures and make notes about them. Notes that could give Jimmy a bit of family history when he got older.

Lori rose to peer over Meg's shoulder and check on her progress. "How are we doing over here?"

Meg sat back in her chair to offer Lori a better view of the pictures she'd spread out on the page. She'd avoided anything as masochistic as photos from her honeymoon, or pictures of her parents. Instead, she'd found something light and fun—a day trip she and Ron had taken to Pike's Peak shortly before they moved away from Colorado. Most of the photos were just of the scenery, and they brought back pleasant memories instead of sad ones.

"What color for the background, do you think?" Meg asked. She held a blue triangle of paper near the pictures, then shook her head—there was so much blue in the sky already. She tried a bright yellow that matched the old jacket she'd been wearing that day, before she bought the red one she wore now. The red jacket that had given her away to Craig.

"That one," Lori said. "The yellow makes a perfect accent for the other colors."

Meg nodded in agreement, and Lori moved on.

She did fine until she got to the last photograph for

the facing page, a picture she'd put off looking at without even realizing it. It was the only photo of Meg and Ron together that day, snapped by an obliging tourist from Florida. Both of Ron's arms were draped in front of her in that proprietary way he had, and his head leaned on top of hers. She'd forgotten his smile. And she'd nearly forgotten what he looked like out of uniform. In the picture, he wore a windbreaker that hadn't proven nearly warm enough for the high elevation of Pike's Peak, even in June.

And she'd forgotten why they went there that day. Ron thought, before they left Colorado, Meg would like to pay a visit to the mountain she'd seen on the horizon nearly every day of her life.

The picture blurred. Meg froze, waiting for the feeling to pass. Ron *had* cared about her. One more thing she'd chosen to forget. Maybe because it was easier to feel anger than to feel pain. She felt a light hand on her shoulder.

"Are you okay?" Lori asked.

Remembering her Lamaze tricks, Meg took a deep breath, then carefully blinked. The tears stayed in. She looked up.

Lori stood over her, but somehow, by some silent signal, she'd made her other three friends disappear. "What is it?"

"I forgot . . ." *I forgot what it was like when it was good.* She couldn't say that. "It's been a while since I looked at his picture."

"Oh, sweetie." Lori bent down nearer. "You can't hide from your memories."

Not this again. She couldn't keep playing the part of the sainted widow. But she couldn't hide from people like Lori forever either. This was too small a town; there would always be people who remembered Ron. Besides, Lori was fast becoming a real friend. Meg took a deep breath, and took a step at pulling off the mask she'd been hiding behind. She looked up at a blurry Lori. "It wasn't always perfect."

Lori didn't flinch. "Of course not, honey. Nothing is."

Meg sniffed. Lori produced a tissue out of nowhere.

"Want to talk?" Lori asked.

Meg shook her head.

"Want a cookie?"

It sounded like she was talking to a two-year-old. Meg let out a spurt of laughter. "A cookie sounds great. You make a terrific mom."

"Oh, I don't know. Eight-and-a-half months old and she's giving me attitude already. Her dad's watching her in the bedroom tonight. I kind of like having the break."

So even Miss Mary Sunshine had her moments. She'd have to tell Crai—

Meg shut out the thought as she waited for Lori to return with not just one chocolate chip cookie, but a plateful. She took a consoling bite. Homemade. Definitely.

"You're sure you don't want to talk?" Lori waved a dismissive hand back toward the kitchen, where she'd apparently banished her other three friends. "They can go. They're here all the time. They'll understand. They know what you've been through."

No one did. No one but Craig.

"It's okay." Meg finished her first cookie. It helped, a little. She must be really shallow. "It's kind of good to have people around."

"You've been trying to do it all yourself, haven't you? It's okay to have some help, you know. All you have to do is ask."

A lump in her throat blocked the next bite of cookie. Lori might be Mary Poppins on the outside, but she could be alarmingly perceptive on the inside.

Kind of a funny way to live your life, Meg. Be nice to the girls at the dress shop, but not too nice. Be friendly with Helen, but not too friendly. And, at all costs, stay away from people who'd known Ron, because—what? They'd find out what a terrible person she really was?

Craig had seen her at her worst, and he didn't think she was terrible. Lori had caught a glimpse of her at a bad moment, and what had she done? Promptly admitted that she wasn't perfect, either. Craig had been right about so many things. Was that why she'd run away from him? Because he had her number? For all her talk about betrayal and independence, what kept making her cringe was the thought of looking him in the eye, knowing he knew so much about her.

And pleasant as the company was tonight, she hadn't stopped thinking about him since she got here.

She felt like a lovesick teenager, but it was for the

best. She missed Craig, but he didn't want to deal with a baby. She knew that. And she wouldn't let herself turn into one of those pitiable women, desperate to have a man for the sole purpose of helping to support a child. She saw enough of that at the Joshua Center. The only thing for her to do was take the lessons she'd learned and pick up her life from here.

Meg finished her second cookie and offered Lori the most convincing smile she could muster. "It's okay. Bring 'em back in."

She got back to work on her album, leaving lots of room below the picture to make some notes about Ron, when she was ready. Craig had been right about that, too, the day he'd put the diaper table together. Jimmy should know about his father.

Craig rang the doorbell of the little white house in the older part of Victory and adopted a nonchalant stance, leaning against the post supporting the porch roof while he waited for a response.

The door opened. Craig folded his arms and drawled, "You report a leak, ma'am?"

"I did not." The middle-aged woman pushed open the screen door. "Just once, I wish you'd come here without having to fix something."

Craig stepped inside and gave his mother a hug. Today, she just might get her wish, if he could manage to come up with the words. "You sure?" he asked. "Nothing I can do while I'm here?" The screen door shut smoothly behind him, and he noticed with satisfaction that it didn't squeak. He'd installed it last summer.

"Not a thing," Mrs. Stovall said. Her brown hair was losing the battle with the gray, and the line of her chin was rounder, less defined than it had been before Craig moved out ten years ago. Coming to see her was always a little like seeing a picture out of focus, until he adjusted; in his mind, she always looked the way she had when he still lived at home. "How about you?" She folded her arms in an imitation of his stance. "Can I get you anything?"

"Got any chocolate cake?" he asked, partly joking, partly hoping. Mostly joking.

"Chocolate cake?" She laughed and led him toward the kitchen. "You must have the wrong house."

"Sorry. Any of those killer brownies, just like Safeway used to make?"

Her smile widened. "Even better." He followed her to the pinewood pantry he'd built two years ago, where she pulled out a clear plastic bowl with a grocery label on top. Craig saw tempting chunks of chocolate inside. "These are new. Bite-size. Have a seat."

Craig sat down at the kitchen table. The white straight-backed chairs weren't the same ones he remembered. Craig doubted he'd ever sat in one of these. He felt a little too big for it, as though it might break under his weight.

His mother set the bowl and a plate in front of him and offered him coffee. He didn't know if that had ever happened before, either. Usually he came in and got busy with some minor fix-it job that needed to be done. If his mother was going to keep living in this tired part of town, her house was going to be the best-maintained one on the block. His visits were usually accomplished without him ever sitting down, and he always left before his stepfather got home.

Craig had the feeling some of the answers to the tangled mess he was in were here in this house. She hadn't moved since Craig was seven. He wondered, for the first time, if she'd insisted on keeping it when she and Ben got married. Everything else was so different after that, but at least their home had stayed the same. Maybe Craig kept the house in good condition as a way of repaying her. Or maybe he hoped his actions said things he couldn't.

It was easier to deal with a house, than whatever it was that was supposed to make it a home.

Mrs. Stovall sat down to join him. Coffee with his mother. Definitely weird. But it was nice to see the warm welcome in her eyes. They were a lighter blue than his, but they were the one thing about her face that remained unchanged by time. "So," she said, "what have you been up to?"

Her pleasure at having him sit down in her kitchen was tangible. Surely he could have done this before. Now would be the perfect time for small talk; instead, he was getting ready to dump his problems into her lap. Some son. But if he beat around the bush, Craig was afraid he'd never get around to what he'd come here to talk about.

"Well," he shoved a handful of hair back from his

forehead, "business is good." Darn. He was stalling anyway. If only he'd finished the cabin by now, so he could bring her the key.

"But that's not what you came here to talk about." The smile dimmed slightly, but the warmth didn't.

"No." He leaned back in his chair, sure it would give way under him. "There's this woman," he blurted. "She's pregnant. It's not mine," he added hastily. At least that was one kind of trouble he'd never caused her. "I think I'm in love with her."

His mother blinked. Twice.

"She's not married or anything. Her husband died a few months ago." Craig stared at his coffee cup. He didn't recognize the sunflower pattern of the mug, either. "I guess what I'm wondering is, could I handle it."

She was still staring at him. He'd sure dumped out a truckload, after ten years of never talking below the surface. "Handle what?"

Here was where the rubber met the road. "Mom, you never told me anything about my dad. I mean, why you split up." He had a hard time explaining the connection, even to himself. How could a father long out of the picture help him solve his current predicament? But he'd sat on the question for years, and something compelled him to ask it now.

Mrs. Stovall looked down and stirred her coffee. "You haven't asked me that since you were about fourteen."

"I gave up. I never got an answer. Except for, 'Sometimes things just don't work out.'"

"You weren't old enough. And by the time you were old enough, you weren't talking to me much."

That was something else they'd never touched on. Instead, they'd slowly built up a cordial relationship after Craig moved out of the house, and then the home improvement projects started.

"Sorry." It was an emotional word, but it was high time he said it. It didn't cover nearly enough.

"Water under the bridge," she said.

Craig risked rocking his chair back on its legs. "So, what about my father? Think I'm old enough now?" He tried to soften it with a grin, but he doubted it was too convincing.

His mother's eyes returned to her coffee cup. "He drank."

Craig could tell those words were emotional too. His chair froze with two legs up off the floor, and his mother raised her eyes.

"He was a good person," she went on, "and I tried to deal with it for a while. But he never stayed sober for very long. By the time you were two years old, I knew there was nothing else I could do, and it wasn't something I wanted you growing up around. He couldn't hold a job, and by the end I was bringing in most of the money anyway. So I left."

Craig lowered his chair back to the floor.

It wasn't any worse than he'd imagined, he supposed. Sometimes vague visions of armed robbery and prison had danced in his head, or the theory that his father dumped his mother for some sleazy exotic dancer. Or that he'd taken one last look at Craig, decided it was more than he could handle, and bailed.

Or, in his teens, he'd envisioned his father as the wronged hero who'd been deserted by his wife. Misunderstood, and therefore the only person who'd be able to understand Craig. Part of him had known it was a lie, but he'd clung to it until he started doing construction work for the city, and found something solid to put his energy into. Then he'd stopped thinking about it. Mostly.

"So what happened to him? Where is he now?"

"I stopped hearing from him when you were about seven," she said. "He tried. He sent a little money for you when he could. I always let him know where you and I were, because we moved quite a few times when you were small. But he remarried after we came to Victory, and that was the last I heard from him."

Craig pulled in a breath, wondering why, after all these years, he still felt a pang of disillusionment. His father had known where he was all this time, and never tried to contact him. It certainly didn't provide any magic key to his current situation. Why had he expected it to?

"He worked on cars," his mother added. "He had a good pair of hands. You inherited that from him."

He managed a grin. "That much I knew." Random thoughts still churned in his head.

"But if you're worried about the rest of it—well, I

don't see any signs that you inherited any of his problems. Was that what you were worried about?"

"Maybe. Was that what *you* were worried about?"

"No."

"Then why didn't you ever tell me?"

She sighed. "A boy needs a father," she said. "I wasn't going to lie to you about what broke us up, but I didn't want to give you any bad impressions either. Maybe I did the wrong thing. But by the time you were old enough to understand, there were—other problems."

"Problems? Me?" Craig tried for an angelic look. It must have been sufficiently ridiculous, because it made her laugh. He reached over and squeezed her hand. "You did fine, Mom. You just had a troublemaker for a kid."

"You turned out all right. I'm proud of you."

Why were things like that so hard to say? The funny thing was, it was nothing either of them didn't already know. Craig had stopped resenting his mother a long time ago. Did she know that? Maybe the answer he'd come here for didn't have anything to do with his long-absent father. Maybe the answer was right here at this kitchen table.

"So," she reminded him, "you started out telling me about this woman."

"It's hard to explain. Her husband died in that Air Force plane crash a few months ago."

"Isn't she the one Helen works with at the pregnancy center?" He'd forgotten how often his mother and Helen talked. "The one who's carrying twins?"

"Twins?" Craig felt his jaw go slack.

"Well, that's what Helen said." His mother shook her head. "I should have known better. She says this girl Megan insists she's only having one baby boy, but she's gotten so big Helen's just sure it has to be twins."

Craig chuckled. "Some things never change."

"Craig, I'm sure she's a nice person, but I know how hard it is to be a single mother. Just be sure she's not trying to take advantage of you."

"It's not like that." Craig ran a hand through his hair again. "In fact, she's pushing me away with both hands."

She raised her eyebrows. "Well, then, you'd better go slow. For both your sakes." Mrs. Stovall fingered the handle of her cup. "Give her time. Women can be very emotional when they're pregnant."

"I noticed that."

"Another thing you need to think about is that after a woman has a baby, that's where her focus is. For the first three months you were all I thought about. Of course, you didn't let me get much sleep, either." Her eyes glimmered slightly. "Your honeymoon would have to wait, probably for quite a while."

Craig squirmed. "That's not what I'm worried about." He picked up his sunflower coffee cup and took a drink for the first time. He'd let it get cool. "I don't know anything about being a father."

"You had an example right here under this roof. You just never gave Ben a chance."

"I know." He'd hardly even seen Ben since he moved away from home, and never for more than a few minutes.

She glanced at the clock. "He'll be home in a little while, if you'd like to stay for dinner."

Craig followed her eyes to the clock. Unlike many other things in this house, it hadn't changed. It was still the same kitschy black cat, with the swinging tail and the moving eyes, that Craig had given her when he was ten.

"I think he'd be glad to see you," his mother prodded. "I think he'd be glad to see how you've grown."

He knew she didn't mean his height or weight. Craig swallowed hard. It was time to stop avoiding things, if he was even going to think about dealing with Meg again.

"Okay," he said. "I think I'd like that."

"Meg," Stephanie waved the phone behind the counter at Rosie's Rags playfully, "it's for you. Some guy named Craig."

Meg nearly dropped the pair of pants she was folding. Stephanie's eyes were positively gleaming, and she felt Kim watching her, too. Neither of the girls had ever bothered to ask who any of her phone calls were from before. But of course, no male had ever called her at the store before either.

With as little ado as possible, Meg walked over and took the phone from Stephanie, then waited pointedly until both of the girls moved a few steps away.

"Hello?" she said. Professional and composed.

"Did you find anyone else for class tonight?" Craig certainly knew how to cut to the chase.

"No," she said. "I thought maybe I'd go by myself or—"

"I'll pick you up at a quarter to seven, if you want me to."

Meg's heart hit the floor and bounced back up into her throat. "Are you sure?"

"That's why I called." His blunt tone was so hard to read. But it was still good to hear his voice. And she had so little to lose.

"Okay."

Meg hung up. It was the last session of class, so at worst, she was in for an uncomfortable three hours.

At best—no, she knew better than to hope. But maybe, if she wanted it, she had one more chance with Craig.

No, not even a chance. A step. Just like Craig had said. One step at a time. But maybe, just maybe, it was time to stop pushing people away. Let things develop, and see where they led.

One step at a time.

"Meg and Craig," Kim said. "That rhymes."

She'd forgotten she had an audience.

Stephanie chimed in: " 'Meg and Craig, sitting in a tree, K-I-S-S-I-N-G . . .' "

Meg was forced to dredge up one of her old school-marm stares.

Chapter Eleven

"**I** was mad at you."

Meg knelt in front of the flat gravestone inscribed with Ron's name. It was the first time she'd been to the cemetery since the funeral.

"We fought before you left and you didn't even come back so we could make up. I guess a part of me's been mad ever since. But I loved you." Meg steadied her voice. "I wasn't sure about that for a while. I think maybe being mad was easier than hurting."

Her eyes wandered to the grass surrounding the stone, which remained a perverse green in spite of the fact that spring was still a few weeks away. The stone hadn't been there at the service, of course. It flitted through Meg's mind how suitable it was that grave markers were made of concrete; seeing it made everything more real. She cleared her throat.

"You have a son," she said. "I don't really know how

you'd feel about that, and I guess I'll never know. His name is Jimmy. He's due in two weeks."

Rocking awkwardly on her knees, Meg slid a cellophane-wrapped bundle of white roses into the metal cone set in the ground above the stone. "These are from your son," she said. "I wanted something blue, but this time of year, they didn't have anything." The roses tottered to one side, and she wished she'd thought to have the stems cut shorter. Meg blinked hard. "I'll never know what you would have said when I told you. What kind of dad you would have been. How it would have all worked out. But there's someone now—" She lowered her eyes to the impossibly green grass underneath her. "I think he cares about me. And I might be in love with him."

It was the first time she'd voiced the thought. What a strange person to tell it to. "I guess I don't need your permission exactly. But before I try, I needed to forgive you. And ask you to forgive me."

Meg stared down at the dates at the stone, struck once again by its finality. She still had no idea what Ron would have said, but she supposed that wasn't the point.

A tear splashed onto the gray cement. With difficulty, Meg rose to her feet and left it there, along with the flowers.

Craig wasn't ready for the reactions that assaulted him when Meg opened the door to her apartment.

She looked bigger. Could a pregnant woman get visibly bigger in a week? Her face looked paler, tired in a way he hadn't seen before. But big or not, pale or not, she was beautiful. Somehow she seemed more real to him, more vivid, like meeting someone he'd only seen from a distance. *Go slow,* his mother had said. If he pushed too hard now, after last week, he might drive her away altogether.

So Craig gave her his friendliest customer-service smile. "How are you?"

"Fine." She gave a tentative smile in return. "How about you?"

"Good." He wanted to reach for her, hold her, and that felt so natural. He kept his hands in his pockets instead. "You look a little tired."

"Thanks a lot." She hefted her chin at him, but the smile didn't leave. Meg picked her purse up off the back of the couch next to the door. "My back's been killing me this afternoon. The doctor warned me to expect it when I saw him Monday. He says the baby's dropped."

"Dropped?"

"It happens in the last couple of weeks. That means he's moving down to . . ."

"Got it." He should have known better than to ask. At least the answer put a little flush in her cheeks.

She joined him outside, closed the door behind her, and turned to face him. "Thanks for doing this," she said.

He forced a lightness into his tone. "Least I could do." Standing this close to her, he felt way too warm in the heavy wool sweater he'd finally remembered to wear for the icy classroom.

As Meg led him away from the apartment he fought the urge to take her arm, give her a hand. She looked like she could use one. *It's good to see you,* he wanted to say, but he bit the words back, afraid to press his luck. It was strange. Much as he loved his mother, it was hard to say affectionate words to her. It was hard *not* to say them to Meg.

I missed you, Meg wanted to say. But Craig seemed to be holding his distance. After last week's drama, she couldn't blame him. What had she expected, that they'd fall into each other's arms? After everything she'd said to him last week? He'd had plenty of time to cool off since then, and think of all the reasons she'd given for them not to get involved. They probably made more sense to him than that brief embrace. Maybe he was just doing this to be nice, or out of some sense of obligation. Or guilt. She knew a lot about that one.

She ventured, "I'm sorry about last week."

"Don't worry about it." His offhand tone didn't give her any clues.

Her back *was* killing her. She'd started to notice it as she left the cemetery, and it seemed to be getting worse, the dull ache gradually sharpening to concentrate on a specific point near the base of her spine. As she trudged alongside Craig toward her apartment complex's parking lot, she could tell he was slowing his pace for her. Meg tried to walk faster.

"How's the work on the church coming along?" she asked. Why had she brought up the church, after what happened there? And how far away was Craig's truck, anyway?

"Oh. Done. I put in a lot of hours this week." He looked down at her with a smile. "The devil makes work for idle hands."

First her back was killing her. Now her knees wanted to buckle under that grin. Suddenly he didn't seem so standoffish. *Do something. Say something.* All she could manage was an insipid smile.

At last, they'd reached his truck. Which meant it was time for the now-familiar ritual of allowing Craig to help her in. Meg inhaled deeply, feeling a strange mix of fear and anticipation as he reached for her arm.

Then it happened. As he boosted her up toward the high seat, the tightness in her back narrowed to a precise point that reached clear through her back to—

The baby.

Automatically, Meg dropped her head and started her rapid, hissing breaths. She felt Craig's arms supporting her, but his voice seemed to come from far away.

"Meg?"

"Megan Reilly," Craig told the woman behind the counter at the hospital, feeling a strange sense of deja vu.

"Craig, I can talk. It's okay."

The same heavy redhead took a look at Meg, who stood with her elbows braced on the counter, and called for a wheelchair. From her new seat, Meg answered questions, fished out her insurance card, and paused to breathe for contractions, all with amazing composure. Apparently, Craig learned with relief, a lot of the paperwork had been done ahead of time.

It wasn't until they started wheeling her toward some forbidden swinging doors to have her "prepped"—Craig didn't want to think about what that meant—that Meg suddenly looked small and scared.

"Wait," Craig said to the orderly pushing the wheelchair. The chair stopped. Meg's eyes met his. They'd never looked bigger or darker. Craig reached for her hand, and she held on to his readily. He crouched down so they were face to face.

"It's okay," he said. "I'll wait right here while they get you ready." He squeezed her hand, aware that he was tottering on the brink of a ledge. "I'll stick around as long as you want me to."

She smiled. "Thanks." And kept her grip on his hand.

Craig took a deep breath and plunged. "Do you want me to call Lori?" He paused. "Or do you want me to stay?"

Meg bit her lip. In Craig's peripheral vision, the orderly behind the chair shifted his feet.

"Call Lori," Meg said.

He should be relieved beyond measure. Instead, Craig felt a sharp twinge of hurt.

"Let her know what's going on," she said. Her eyes held on to his. "But I want you to stay."

Both of them let out the same long, slow breath.

Craig squeezed her hand again, let go, and watched Meg vanish behind the ugly green swinging doors. He stood stock still, staring at those doors until they came to a complete rest. When they stopped, Craig leaned against the wall behind him, struck by a totally unfamiliar sensation.

He felt like he was going to pass out.

Another contraction hit, the pressure at her back so ruthless it was all Meg could do not to push. She signaled Craig, who led her through another spate of deep breaths. Her legs started to tingle again. By now, she'd breathed into a paper bag several times to control the hyperventilating.

The pressure eased, and Meg relaxed against the pillows. It had all started out so innocuously. The contractions had been sharp, but nothing she couldn't handle for the thirty seconds or so that they lasted. In between, she and Craig whiled away the time watching the television set mounted from the ceiling. She'd felt bad for even asking Craig to stay, because the whole thing had been pretty dull. For the first three hours.

Then, about two hours ago, the contractions had gotten relentless. The last time the nurse checked, Meg had still been nowhere near the final phase of labor, but the past hour had been a pure onslaught.

Another one. Meg abandoned all thoughts of Lamaze and let go. She cried out until the contraction subsided.

"Honey." She felt Craig's fingers, cool against the back of her neck, as the pain faded. "It's okay."

She hadn't caught her breath yet when the next one hit. *Not again.* Meg gasped once and cried out again.

Craig felt helpless as he let her shout, her hand clenched hard around his. He stroked her hair, but he wasn't sure if she even knew he was there. At last her cries stopped, and she went limp against the pillow. He tried to think of something comforting to say, something encouraging.

She tensed, and he could tell it was coming again. This time her eyes met his. "Craig—"

The panic he saw there made his blood run cold. He didn't know what was happening, but he knew he couldn't let it go on. He hadn't been ready for anything like this. But that didn't matter. He had to get a grip and do what he was there to do.

"Meg." She drew in a breath, and he could see she was about to cry out again. He turned her head toward him and fixed his eyes on hers. "Stay with me. You can do this." He held three fingers in front of her, signaling the number for the next set of breaths, the way they'd done in class.

She started counting out the breaths with him. Her hand remained tight around his, but her eyes lost that wild, panicked look.

It was the longest contraction yet. When it was over, Meg slumped again. Craig felt as wrung out as she looked, and he wasn't the one with the labor pains. They'd been at this for hours, and somewhere in that time it had become undeniably clear to him. He loved Meg. The thought of anything happening to her terrified him. But that was exactly why he had to keep a cool head, even as he did everything he could for her with no holds barred. He could worry about his own feelings later. Right now, what mattered was getting her through this, no matter how much it took out of him.

He cast his eyes around just as their nurse returned, apparently brought back by the last round of yelps. She'd been dropping in now and then to check on them, but Craig had been surprised to find how much of the labor process was left to the patient and her coach.

"Can we check her again?" He made his voice brusque, businesslike, to cover the fear he felt. "She's got to be getting close by now."

The nurse, a gray-haired veteran, nodded.

"Stick with it," he told Meg, aware that they were due for the next onslaught. "Remember to breathe."

"Sorry." She managed a wan smile. "But it sure felt good to yell."

"I'll bet. I would have been yelling a long time ago."

"Well, you know what they say about men—" She tensed again. Craig kept his eyes on hers through the spate of panting breaths, determined not to let her get away from him again.

When the contraction was over, the nurse stepped away from the foot of the bed and announced in her raspy voice, "Six centimeters."

Craig stared at her. "That's out of ten?"

The nurse sent him a glare. "Yes, out of ten. Weren't you paying attention in Lamaze class?"

"Of course I was," Craig flared back. "I just hoped—"

"Uh, Craig?" Meg's grip tightened once more, bringing his attention back where it belonged. He held up the fingers of his free hand. Two breaths. Now, three. Change it up, give her something to focus on, until she sank back once again, completely limp. Her hair was damp against the pillow. Craig rested a hand on her forehead.

The nurse's expression softened. "You know, we're still at a stage where you could have some pain medication. If your labor starts to progress soon, we might get too close to delivery."

Meg hesitated. When they'd asked her at the front desk, a few hours or a few years ago, she'd said she wanted her delivery to be as natural as possible. Since then, they'd already strapped a monitor around her considerable belly to keep an eye on the baby's heart rate.

The nurse said, "It's just something to help you relax between contractions. If you want."

Meg had to endure another contraction before she could answer.

When it was over, she looked at Craig's exhausted face. "It's up to you, honey," he said. "They don't give grades on this stuff." His tone was neutral, but his features showed a strain she'd never seen before, not on anyone. She'd dragged him into a nightmare. Finally she nodded.

At first, the drugs helped. The nurse lowered the bed to let her lie down, and Meg drifted between the contractions. They weren't much less intense, but somehow they mattered less, and in between, she felt as if she were floating, probably dozing. She had no idea how much time went by. She was aware, most of all, of Craig's voice, talking to her softly; sometimes, it seemed, nonsensically. And of his hand, never letting go of hers. When she tried to answer him, she couldn't tell if she spoke out loud or just heard the words in her mind. She remembered a moment when he was stroking her hair, her hand still in his, when she looked into his eyes and felt an incredible moment of peace and safety. She knew it would be all right. She might have said something then.

Some time after that, it changed. The pain reached in and found her full force, even through the haze of the medication. She heard voices around her, talking about the baby's heart rate, and getting her doctor in. She heard the word "distress."

Craig's face leaned in close to hers. "Honey, they're getting ready to do a C-section. It'll be okay . . ."

Meg doubled over for another contraction, and Craig's hand was gone.

The bed was moving. No, it wasn't a bed any more. A gurney. People surrounded her, wheeling her rapidly down a corridor, and she saw her feet go through a set of metal swinging doors ahead of her. It was like a nightmare, or something out of a thousand television episodes. It couldn't be real.

Except that the pain was real. She let the cries come again, with no one there to guide her through the pain. The gurney came to a halt and the people stopped moving. The chattering didn't stop, but no one seemed to be talking to her. Where was Craig? At last she found a face focused on hers, with a pair of unfamiliar brown eyes showing above a blue paper mask.

"Is the baby all right?" she asked.

"Dr. Razo will be here soon." It was a male voice, compassionate and far too young. Meg noticed he hadn't answered her question. "We need to do the anesthesia now. We're going to give you a shot. . . ."

No more drugs, she wanted to say, but a vicious contraction took the words away. When it was over, a new, terse voice ordered her to lie on her side and bend her spine. Meg felt the needle. As soon as it was gone, multiple hands turned her onto her back.

"Jimmy," she murmured, and tried for a fervent prayer, but her mind couldn't focus. Nothing made sense.

The pain stopped. But what about her baby? She tried to ask, and got soothing responses from blue-masked faces, but no real answers. Her eyes wouldn't stay open. When she did open them she saw a white sheet hanging over her midsection, blocking her view of her lower body. Tugging sensations at her stomach. Darkness.

And then, a baby's cry.

She tried to pull upright, and dozens of hands came

to restrain her. She watched a gowned figure carry him to the other side of the room, taking him away from her.

The dark haze sucked her back down.

Meg woke to dim lights. It took her several minutes to recognize the room where she'd spent so much time with Craig, counting out all those breaths. All for what? She was alone, with no baby in sight. A white clock on the opposite wall pointed to a time shortly after three-thirty. Day or night? She had no idea. And there was no one to ask.

Where was Jimmy? And where had Craig gone?

"Where's my baby?" she asked the petite dark-haired nurse who came in a few minutes later. She was the first person Meg had seen without a mask since this nightmare had begun in earnest.

The nurse looked uncertain. "I'll have to check for you," she said, and began squeezing Meg's legs, asking if she felt anything. She seemed satisfied with the responses, but she wasn't meeting Meg's eyes. It all felt wrong, desperately wrong.

The nurse checked her blood pressure and left. Meg waited.

And waited. She tried to get up, but an IV tugged at her arm, and she could barely move her legs. The room was dim, but the hallway beyond was bright; it must be night. Which night?

She glanced next to her and found controls mounted

on one arm of the bed. Meg found the signal to ring for a nurse and pressed it. Nothing.

Four o'clock came and went. Meg's foreboding grew. She shut her eyes and clung to the dim memory of her baby's cry. Tears pricked behind her eyes, grew huge and leaked out. She'd panicked. She'd failed. And she'd never even seen Jimmy's face.

Chapter Twelve

"**S**omeone wants to see you."

Meg jerked and felt a sharp pain in her abdomen. Had she slept? Again?

The room was still dim. Craig stood over her, gently lowering a tightly-wrapped bundle onto the pillow next to her head. Meg turned with difficulty and saw a small, scrunched face, framed by dark hair, nestled into a hospital-issue striped blanket. His eyes squinched and he made snuffling noises. He looked as confused as she felt.

"Jimmy?" Meg said incredulously. She touched one soft, ruddy cheek. She looked up at Craig, afraid this was some kind of trick to pacify her. "Is he really mine?"

"You have to ask, with all that dark hair?" He stroked the downy waves that covered the baby's head. Craig's hand looked big and rough, as large as the little head under it, but very gentle. Then he looked at Meg, his gaze focusing above her eyes, near the top of her head.

For a moment she thought he would touch her hair, too. But he didn't.

"Is he okay?"

"Perfect." With one finger, Craig traced the baby's chin. He paused at a strawberry-colored patch on Jimmy's skin. "This is where he got stuck, they told me. He was facing the wrong way and that's why you weren't getting anywhere. His heart rate dropped, just for a few seconds, but that was enough to give them a reason to do the Caesarian."

Meg watched Jimmy's lips working. He squirmed. He probably wanted his arms out of the tight bundle they had him wrapped in. She reached up to loosen the blanket. As soon as she freed him, his arms flailed, and he hit himself in the face.

Craig said, "That's his Three Stooges routine. He smacks himself a lot." She studied Craig, but his eyes were back on Jimmy. "I had a lot of time to watch him," he said. "It took a while. They had to clean him up, check him over. They wanted to be sure his lungs were okay, because he was a little early. But everything's perfect."

Meg held down the flailing arms, and Jimmy seemed to calm a little. She searched his tiny face, unable to tell if his round, bewildered eyes were actually focused on her. She put her right little finger into his palm, and he grasped it tightly. After all the books she'd read, she knew it was just a reflex, but it was the most gratifying reflex Meg had ever known.

"How do you feel?" Craig asked.

She smiled faintly, still barely able to believe this was real. "Sore. Confused. Relieved. I really thought he might—" She bit her lip. The warm, solid reality was still gripping her finger. "Where did you go? When I was having him, I mean?"

"They made me change into scrubs before I could go in the operating room."

"You were there?"

He nodded. "You didn't know me. By the time I got there . . . well, whatever they gave you before the surgery, I guess it was pretty potent."

So he'd been there, wearing a blue mask just like everyone else. Safety and comfort had been there all along and she hadn't even known.

But there was something wrong in the twist of Craig's smile. Meg frowned as a vague recollection hit her. She remembered those moments of contentment before the biggest siege of pain hit. "Did I say something? When I was under the anesthetic?"

"Don't worry about it." Craig's hand hovered near hers, then offered a finger for Jimmy's other hand to grasp. It did, tenaciously, and for the moment the three of them were linked. "You did a great job."

"I lost it." Had she called him every name in the book? Or had she said something else, something even more embarrassing, that kept Craig from meeting her eyes? "I panicked."

"No grades, remember? What matters is how it all

turns out." Craig's voice came out husky. "Just look at him."

Meg did, and Craig watched as that unguarded softness he'd so rarely seen filled her features. She started to count Jimmy's fingers, just the way the nurse had told him she'd do. He let go of the baby's hand, leaving Meg free to complete the inventory.

They made a beautiful pair, with those matching dark heads. If it wasn't for all that thick hair, he didn't know if he could have told Jimmy apart from any other newborn baby, but he was still the most amazing thing Craig had ever seen.

In the past couple of hours, while Meg slept, Craig had stood by and watched while the nurses and doctors cleaned him up and checked him over, fascinated by all his small movements and reactions. He wouldn't have thought a person could be so small, yet so complete.

Then they'd handed him to Craig. He hadn't expected that. He shifted the near-weightless bundle awkwardly, trying to support him, and the baby jerked as if in alarm. "Is he okay?" Craig gathered Jimmy closer against his chest to steady him.

"That's the startle reflex." The crusty nurse from the labor room had stuck with them through the whole process, though Craig was sure her work shift must be over by now. "They've been floating inside their mother for nine months. It just takes some time to get used to things."

"Easy, guy," Craig said, and Jimmy swatted himself in the face.

"He knows your voice," the nurse said.

"What?"

"They can hear before they're born, didn't you know that?" Her voice held some of that old disapproval. "From five or six months on."

He'd met Meg when she was seven months pregnant.

Now, looking down at Meg and Jimmy, Craig felt a sharp pang. He had no idea how, or if, he fit into the picture. It wasn't his baby. And in spite of all the plans he'd begun to dream up in his own head, Meg had never said she'd changed her mind about wanting him in their lives. Not when she wasn't under the influence of painkillers, anyway.

"I'll call Lori," he said. "I phoned when we first got here, but that was before everything got out of hand. I'm sure she'll be here to see you tomorrow."

Craig wondered if she'd ask if he was coming, too. But she didn't. So he stood.

Meg caught his hand and squeezed it. "Thanks for everything."

He winced. "Could you do that with my other hand, please?"

Meg loosened her grip and looked down at his hand. Craig hadn't noticed the bruises himself until now, the outer edges of his knuckles tender and discolored from hours of being clutched through her contractions. Meg looked up, and the concern in her dark eyes sent a shot through him. "I'm sorry."

"Don't be." He maintained his smile. "I wouldn't have traded places with you."

"I couldn't have done it without you," she said.

He felt like someone had poked his insides with a big, sharp stick. "Honey, you did."

He let go of her hand and stepped back.

Craig took one more look at the two dark heads on the bed. One of them was still trying to get his bearings; one studied him with an unreadable look that threatened to tear him in two. He had to get out, quick. The delivery had taken just about everything he had. He'd done his part, and now it was time to go. And wait. It was nearly five in the morning, no time for weighty questions about where they'd go from here.

Craig ran a hand lightly, one more time, over Jimmy's soft head.

"He's had a bottle," he told her. "I gave it to him."

And he left her there, cradling another man's baby in her arms.

Chapter Thirteen

Jimmy was frantic. Meg had tried nursing, then she'd tried giving him a bottle, but nothing stopped him from sobbing and flailing his hands. If he'd had the coordination, she was sure he would have wrung them.

"Try the pacifier again," Lori suggested.

He took it and slurped with wild enthusiasm, as if he hadn't refused it five minutes ago. She had no way of telling how long her luck would hold, so Meg took advantage of the brief silence. "It's awfully nice of you to come in on your lunch hour."

"Are you kidding? I would've been down here before work, if Craig called me half an hour earlier."

The pacifier wobbled, and Meg quickly held it in place. "So, what time did he call?" She tried to keep her tone casual.

"Around seven-thirty."

Meg ventured to finger a lock of dark hair above

Jimmy's soft ear. She would have sworn his hair had grown longer, just since last night.

"Craig was that gorgeous guy at the mall, right? You didn't tell me *he* was your Lamaze classmate. How did you manage—"

A nurse walked in, bearing a vase of bright yellow flowers. Meg must have seen five different nurses in here since the sun came up; it was hard to imagine they'd been so scarce last night.

In a flash Lori had cleared the small night table next to the bed, dumping her own purse onto the chair where she'd just been sitting. The nurse left, and Lori angled the front of the arrangement toward Meg. "Can you see them okay?"

Meg nodded. "Who are they from?" Her eyes fixed on the little envelope poking out of the arrangement on a plastic holder.

Lori freed the square envelope and glanced at Meg for permission to open it. Meg nodded; she didn't want to risk disturbing Jimmy just when she'd gotten him settled. Lori pulled out the card, read it and grinned. "Rosie, Stephanie, and Kim. I called your store from the office to pass the word along. They sure got these out quick. I'll bet they called the florist at the gift shop down in the lobby—Meg? What's wrong?"

Meg tore her stare away from the flowers. "Nothing. Just hormones."

"You were expecting the flowers to be from someone else, weren't you?"

"No."

"Hoping?"

"I don't know." Meg looked down at Jimmy. Somehow, miraculously, he'd fallen asleep. She gathered him closer.

"Craig?" Lori's voice turned soft. Reluctantly, Meg nodded. Lori dumped her purse from the chair to the floor and sat down. "Tell me about it."

"There's not much to tell." Meg tweaked the wisp of hair above Jimmy's ear again. The little guy was practically working on his first set of sideburns. "We were just friends, then it—got complicated." She tried to sound normal, but her voice quavered.

"Just friends? I don't think so. The guy stayed here with you *all night*. A man doesn't go through all this—" Lori gestured around the hospital room "—unless he cares. A lot."

"I put him through the wringer. And not just last night."

"He'll be here. You watch." Lori stood. "I've gotta get back to work, sweetie. I'll see you soon." Her eyes sparkled as she picked up her purse. "But I'll bet Craig gets here first."

Meg smiled weakly. "I hope so."

It seemed like a lot to hope for. She'd put Craig through one ordeal after another. She thought about the Lamaze classes, and that long, horrible discussion when she'd vowed not to need anyone ever again. And still he'd come back and seen her through the delivery.

Okay. Either Craig was coming back for sure, or he was headed for the nearest foreign border.

Dinner time came and went—another sumptuous, post-Caesarian meal of broth and Jell-O—and she still hadn't heard from Craig.

Jimmy gave her refuge. When he was awake, he occupied Meg's full attention, except for those fleeting moments when she found herself distracted by his dark hair and blue eyes. She'd known her baby would be born with blue eyes, and she knew their color could change within weeks. And it was only natural that Meg's brunette genes would dominate, since Ron's coloring had been light.

There was no reason at all for a dark-haired, blue-eyed baby to make her think of Craig.

Of course, when her baby tried to cram both of his fists into his mouth at once, the way he was doing right now, he was all Jimmy. He lay in a wheeled crib alongside her bed, and by this time Meg was certain he needed a haircut.

She propped herself up awkwardly over the rail of her hospital bed, trying to capture the moment with the disposable camera Lori had brought yesterday. She'd used up most of the film already; Jimmy seemed to change every minute, and she didn't want to miss any of it. Sitting halfway up to take the pictures played havoc with her sore stomach muscles, but at least the nurses had disconnected her from all the IV tubes. Meg hooked her elbows tenaciously over the rail and leaned forward a little more, peering at Jimmy through the little viewfinder. He looked up at her through half-lidded eyes over the too-long, soggy sleeves of his hospital shirt, and she snapped the photo. Success.

"Are you supposed to be doing that?"

Meg twisted toward the sound of Craig's voice, earning a fresh twinge from her belly muscles. She lowered the camera, but the picture of him standing in the doorway would live in her mind forever. A denim jacket replaced the familiar beige down vest, and the blue fabric made the color of his eyes even more vivid than usual. He held several boxes under his arm, but Meg barely noticed. She couldn't look away from his face.

She wanted to jump up and grab him, but it wasn't just her stitches that stopped her. Whatever he'd come back for, it was serious, and the weight of his gaze set her heartbeat slamming in her throat. Meg forced herself to take a long deep breath and waited to find out what his somber expression meant.

Craig took another step into the room. "Shouldn't you be lying down?"

"Oh." Meg realized that her half-crouching position allowed the loose hospital gown to shift around her, exposing all kinds of skin she usually kept covered. She eased into a sitting position and pulled the bed sheet up over her thighs. Then she tugged it up a little more to cover the shape of her still-large, post-pregnancy stomach. At least they'd let her take a shower this afternoon.

Craig walked up to the little wheeled tray next to the bed, where she'd been having her liquid meals. He laid boxes down on the tray, one by one. "Scrabble. Yahtzee. Chinese checkers." As if he were laying out the instruments for an operation. "And a Koontz book." He laid a paperback on the top of the stack. Had she told him she liked Dean Koontz? "They told me you don't get out of here until day after tomorrow. I thought the time might be going pretty slow."

Meg stared at the pile. "Thanks." It came out sounding like a question. She glanced up to read his expression, but he was stepping toward Jimmy's wheeled crib.

Craig said, "So how's Moe?"

It took her a minute. Moe, as in Larry, Curly, and Moe, the Three Stooges. "He's moved on from hitting himself to trying to eat his own fingers."

Craig ran a fingertip lightly over the baby's cheek. Meg expected Jimmy to squawk, but he didn't.

It was hard to look at Meg, to know what to say, so Craig took an extra moment to study Jimmy. That was even harder. The baby slurped contentedly away on a sleeve, his eyes closed. Craig had felt that baby move inside Meg, had been there when he was born. The nurse said he recognized Craig's voice, but Craig was supposed to wait. Go slow. Give her time.

He couldn't.

Craig looked up at her and sucked in a deep breath.

"Meg, I'm not good at being patient. I've tried being a friend. I've tried playing nursemaid. But I can't."

"What do you mean?"

Craig gripped the metal rail at the top of the rolling crib. "I know I should give you more time, but heck, I can't even stay away from you for one day while you're in the hospital."

Her luminous dark eyes looked at him as if he were certifiably insane. She needed him, whether she knew it or not, but he didn't know if he could convince her of that.

He paced to avoid her incredulous stare. "I know I shouldn't put any pressure on you. But leaving the two of you here last night—it's the hardest thing I've ever done. You're too important to me. I thought I'd never want a family. Now you're all I want. Both of you."

There wasn't much room to pace. He'd returned to the head of the bed. Craig glanced first at a sleeping Jimmy, then took a deep breath and met the eyes of the woman he'd just given the power to break his heart.

He went for broke. "I'm sorry, Meg. I can't wait. I want to know if you'll marry me."

Huge tears shone in her eyes. And he'd hoped he'd never see her cry again.

Meg said, "Are you crazy?"

He stood his ground. "Yeah. I am."

She grabbed his hand. And pulled. Craig stumbled off-balance as a hospital-bound woman nearly yanked him off his feet. He caught the side rail of her bed just before he fell on her.

"I thought you'd never ask," she said. "That was one long speech."

"Okay." Craig sat down on the edge of the bed, and Meg braced her belly for the expected twinge. He must weigh close to two hundred pounds, but the mattress dipped so gently, it didn't even jar her tender abdomen. "Is that a yes?"

"I told you I wanted to take care of myself," Meg said. "I never wanted to need anyone again."

His hand, so much larger than hers, was absolutely still.

"I guess that's because I never wanted to *lose* anyone again," she said. "And I almost did anyway." Meg traced the hard, firm texture of Craig's palm. It felt so good to touch him. Not just by accident, or for a Lamaze class exercise, but just because she wanted to.

"Of course it's a yes," she told him. "If I said no I'd be crazier than you are."

Meg pulled at his hand again, and this time he understood what she wanted. He leaned in and kissed her. Slowly. The sense of connection was immediate. Meg put her arms around him, pulling him closer, amazed to find this need in herself, one she'd never felt until those first kisses with Craig. Thought deserted her as she tipped her head back, allowing him all the access he wanted. But Craig wouldn't be rushed. His lips lingered over hers, and she had the feeling of being truly savored.

Meg let herself melt, like the snowflakes that had

fallen the first night they kissed. This time there was no need to pull back, to try to deny what she felt. He knew all her worst secrets, and still he wanted to spend his life with her.

When his lips left hers, she asked, "Craig, what did I say when I was under the anesthetic? Before everything went haywire?"

He glanced down at their hands, still joined together. "You said a lot of things."

"Did I say I love you?"

His eyes darted to hers with a smile. "Well, yeah. But I make it a point never to take a woman too seriously when she's on drugs."

She tightened her hand around his. "I'm not on drugs now," she said.

"And?"

Meg held his hand between both of hers and smiled. "And . . . I have a confession to make."

Epilogue

"The first thing to know about tiling a floor," Craig said, "is to start laying the tile in the most visible part of the room. A lot of people don't think of that. You want to plan it so the odd-sized pieces, the ones you have to cut to fit, end up at the sides where they're less conspicuous."

"Boo wah," Jimmy replied from his vantage point just outside the bathroom door. The playpen stood in the middle of the hallway, where the ten-month-old could pull up and get a full view of Craig's progress as he re-tiled the bathroom.

"You got it." Craig grinned at his captive audience. With Craig kneeling on the floor, Jimmy was just about at eye level. And for the moment, his round eyes seemed perfectly content to watch the show. Better than cartoons.

"You're brainwashing him," Meg said when she returned a short time later.

"Absolutely." Craig winked up at her. "He's getting a set of plastic tools for his first birthday. You know that."

Meg stood in the hallway with an armload of fat binders, her lips curved up in a tolerant smile. A floor full of tools and a playpen blocked Craig's way to her, so instead of getting up from his knees, he took advantage of the view of her long legs. "You do know," Meg said, "you don't have to renovate this whole house the first year we're married."

"The devil makes work for idle hands," he reminded her lightly.

He teased her, but in reality, he never failed to appreciate Meg's patience. She'd been more than tolerant when he'd taken her to see this house for the first time. Of course Craig's dream home had to be a fixer-upper. It dated back to the thirties, with plenty of built-in shelves, odd nooks and crannies, and a lot of character. It also needed a lot of work. Fortunately, like him, Meg had been excited by the possibilities.

She tried to navigate around the playpen with her arms full, and Craig stood, reaching across the corner of the playpen to take the load of binders. "Those are the samples for the house on Tatum Street," she said. "Carpet, paint . . . do you think we should pick out drapes, too?"

"What do you think?" He'd quickly learned to rely on Meg's judgment. Her choices on his last project had brought the price of the house up by several thousand dollars when they sold it.

Meg bit her lip as she considered. "People like to pick

their own drapes," she decided, her voice reluctant, then bent to scoop up Jimmy. She sighed, and her face lit up. Her expression took on that soft glow whenever she held him, as if she were enjoying a cool drink of water after a hot day. It made her look even more beautiful.

Craig eyed a plastic shopping bag hanging on her arm. "What's in there? Something from Rosie's Rags?"

She grinned. "I had to celebrate. I made a discovery today. I'm finally back down to my old size." She scuttled past him toward the nursery with Jimmy in her arms.

That night, just as Meg was drifting off to sleep, Craig said, "You know, you might not want to get too used to wearing your old size."

Meg's head rested on Craig's shoulder, one arm draped across his chest. "Hm?" she murmured drowsily.

"I was thinking. Right now you're stuck here with two guys. . . ." Craig ran a finger lightly over her shoulder and down her arm. "You want to try for a girl next time?"

That woke her up. She lifted her head, trying to make out his expression in the darkness. "Seriously?" It was the first time Craig had come right out and mentioned having another child, although both of them avoided using the third bedroom for anything but temporary storage.

"Sure. I mean, when you're ready. If it's what you want."

Meg debated in silence. Finally, she said, "It's a trick."

"What?"

"Girl, my foot. You want another boy so you can raise a work crew."

"What makes you think I won't stick a hammer into my little girl's hand?"

Meg considered. "What makes you think I won't teach Jimmy to bake chocolate cake?"

Craig tangled a hand lazily through her hair. "Okay by me. I told you, I never say no to chocolate cake."

Meg nestled her head back down against Craig's chest, relishing the sound of his heartbeat as she drifted back down toward sleep. The deep sense of contentment was no longer new to her, but she never ceased to marvel at it. Once, she'd thought all she wanted was to take care of herself and her son. Instead, she'd found so much more than she'd ever hoped for—a man with loving hands to build a home, and a loving heart to build a family.